GHOSTLANDS

Ghostlands

Stephen Elboz

OXFORD
UNIVERSITY PRESS

OXFORD
UNIVERSITY PRESS

Great Clarendon Street, Oxford OX2 6DP

Oxford University Press is a department of the University of Oxford.
It furthers the University's objective of excellence in research, scholarship,
and education by publishing worldwide in

Oxford New York

Auckland Bangkok Buenos Aires
Cape Town Chennai Dar es Salaam Delhi Hong Kong Istanbul
Karachi Kolkata Kuala Lumpur Madrid Melbourne Mexico City Mumbai
Nairobi São Paulo Shanghai Taipei Tokyo Toronto

Oxford is a registered trade mark of Oxford University Press
in the UK and in certain other countries

British Library Cataloguing in Publication Data available

ISBN 0 19 275228 6

1 3 5 7 9 10 8 6 4 2

Typeset by AFS Image Setters Ltd, Glasgow

Printed in Great Britain by
Cox & Wyman Ltd, Reading, Berkshire

For David Walton

Prologue

The letter arrived quite unexpectedly. It almost sneaked its way into the Niles's household, lurking amongst the usual bills and junk mail.

Mr Niles brought the post back to the breakfast table, shuffling through it like playing cards. Ewan watched his father pause at the unfamiliar white envelope, frowning at it for a while before ripping it open. Inside was a single sheet of writing-paper so thin it crackled in his hands; and through it Ewan glimpsed his father's finger-tips, as well as a block of dense spiky writing in reverse.

Mr Niles looked puzzled. His eyes returned to the beginning of the letter to re-read more slowly, his lips moving in time to the words; not that Ewan could make any sense of what he mouthed.

Ewan's mother watched too, sipping tea from her mug, the one with 'The Boss' emblazoned upon it. She was wearing a big baggy T-shirt with a large fluffy bunny on the front, which Ewan found mildly embarrassing, even though nobody else saw it as she wore it in bed.

'What is it, love?' she asked.

Mr Niles looked up, still looking puzzled. 'It's this letter,' he said needlessly. 'It's from my old godfather.'

'Never knew you had a godfather,' said Mrs Niles as if stumbling across an undisclosed family secret.

'I'd all but forgotten about him myself,' admitted her

husband. 'He seemed such an old man to me even then, but very brainy. Hugh Malthus—*Doctor* Hugh Malthus. My dad used to do work for him.'

'Huh, back in the good old days, eh, Dad?' grunted Ewan.

'Not *so* long ago,' said Mr Niles, pulling in his belly and pretending to be hurt by the remark. 'I was best friends with the doctor's son for a while.' He chuckled, remembering. 'A wild case if ever there was one. Used to get up to some real tricks.'

'What happened to him?' asked Ewan.

Mr Niles shrugged. 'There was an accident and he was killed. After that the doctor turned into a bit of a recluse and refused to see people. Now, after all this time, he's written me a letter.' Ewan found the letter being offered to him across the table. 'He wants you to go and stay with him in the school holidays.'

'No, thank you,' replied Ewan without even considering, and crisply polite, as if refusing another piece of toast or some other small kindness.

'Come on, Ewan, you can't just say no like that,' insisted Mr Niles. 'What a wonderful opportunity. As I remember, the doctor has this great big rambling house surrounded by beautiful countryside; and he's very keen on your going. Here, read for yourself.'

'I don't care what it says,' said Ewan, taking the letter without the slightest intention of doing anything with it, apart from shoving it into some dark corner. 'I'm not being packed off to the middle of nowhere with someone I've never met before and—'

Something fluttered free of the envelope. Mr Niles picked it up saying, 'It's a train ticket,' and he whistled. 'First class.'

2

'First class?' cried Ewan, snatching it from his father's hand to see for himself.

It was probably then that Ewan had his change of mind.

Chapter One

Two weeks after the arrival of the mysterious invitation from Dr Malthus, Ewan found himself aboard a speeding train, feeling both excited and anxious by the thought of what lay at the end of his journey. His seat was wide and comfortable and, settling back into it, he watched the world fly by.

With pleasing uniformity of speed, the slick InterCity cut across open fields, swaying and chattering along its lines. Steadily the sun climbed higher, losing its early morning haziness, until at last, at each long sweeping bend, dazzling flashes of sunlight were reflected from the windows of the rear carriages. Ewan, his forehead pressed up against the glass, decided it was like a dance: the farms and woodland waltzing by, slowly pirouetting into the wings. It was a show to be watched, and he enjoyed it almost as much as the looks cast his way from his fellow first-class passengers—expensively suited businessmen and women for the most part—slyly peering at him from behind their copies of the *Financial Times*, which, as a rule, were held six inches before the nose like a personal wall. Ewan found himself carefully scrutinized, along with his comics and sweets, all neatly arranged on the table before him. And when the ticket-inspector came, Ewan sensed irritation from his fellow passengers when everything proved in order. Triumphantly he smiled at all the stiffly raised newspapers.

At last they pulled into the city and the boy was quickly forgotten as the train emptied and the platform swarmed with purposeful people. Nobody thought to help Ewan with his case and the platform was practically deserted when he finally managed to get himself and his luggage off. Now, as he stood wondering what to do next, his parents' advice struck him as curiously contradictory. 'Ask, if you're lost,' his father had said. 'Don't talk to strangers,' his mother had warned. Ewan sighed. *Just what is a body supposed to do?*

At that moment he heard the swiftly approaching *click-clack-click* of high-heeled shoes and turned. The shoes in question, he saw, were cherry red—as red in fact as the wearer's lipstick. The woman swayed as she walked, a slight totter caused by the heels, her cotton dress restlessly waving and fluttering about her knees. She wore a simple straw hat and white elbow-length gloves; and over the crook of her arm she carried an enormous handbag made of some kind of tapestry, with handles of carved horn. If she had noticed Ewan, she had deemed him unworthy of her interest, carrying herself past him with such confidence that there was something quite intimidating about her.

'E-excuse me,' began Ewan nervously.

'Y-e-s?' The woman's intense gaze swooped down at him: two ice-blue eyes widening behind heavily framed spectacles.

Ewan blinked at his shoes in order to avoid the relentlessness of her stare. 'I was wondering. That is, could you tell me . . . please . . . which platform I go to to catch the train to Gr-Gribbage Holt?'

'*Gribbage Holt?*' A note of curiosity crept into the

5

woman's voice. 'How fortunate. As it so happens that is *my* train. I suggest you follow me and I will put you on the *right track*.' She laughed brightly, but Ewan didn't because he hadn't realized it was a joke.

She walked on before he could thank her, swaying ever so slightly on those blood-red heels, her handbag-carrying arm working in time with the lower half of her body. Ewan struggled with his case, bumping it down the stairs to a platform at a lower level: in fact it was underground and permanently lit with neon strip lights. The train stood waiting. No gleaming InterCity this time, but a multiple-unit that had obviously seen better days—yet grandly bore the name, *The Gribbage Flyer*. The woman lingered at the bottom of the stairs until Ewan had bounced his case off the final step.

'This is it,' she said, regally waving a gloved hand at the train. 'You'll find room in one of the end carriages, the front's reserved for first class.'

'That's okay,' said Ewan, 'I'm travelling first class.'

The woman seemed mildly taken aback at this, but before she could enquire further a carriage door flew open and a group of women burst out, all squawking like parrots and, Ewan noted, all carrying similar cavernous handbags to his guide's.

'Over here, Phyllis!'

'Phyl-lis. Yoo-hoo!'

'Dah-ling.'

The woman spread a hand at the base of her throat then waved at them in mock dismissal. 'Girls . . . girls, I've only been away five minutes.'

'But we thought you lost; and the city's such a big place for a country gal like you to get lost in.'

6

Smiling radiantly, the woman allowed herself to be swept up by her admirers and be borne on to the train. Ewan followed, lugging his case.

The moment he entered, the women fell silent, staring at him coldly. Ewan felt they might even mob him and drive him out, like a bird that strays into another's territory. Nobody else was in that particular carriage and the women obviously considered it as good as theirs.

'Apparently,' Phyllis told her group in not too discreet a whisper, '*he's* first class too. But we won't allow it to spoil our own little fun, shall we, girls? We shall still have a delicious time together.'

Her words set into motion a whole new zoo-load of squawks and coos.

Finding a place away from them on the other side of the gangway, Ewan sat down heavily. His seat was lumpy and rather worn, and he could feel the springs move beneath him like dislocated bones, poking into him at every opportunity. If this was first class, he wondered what the rest of the train was like.

Just then the driver appeared, respectfully removing his cap and smoothing down his hair, even though it wasn't standing up and he didn't have much of it. 'Ah, Mrs Flight,' he said to the woman in red shoes. 'You've found your way to us at last. Your ladies were growing concerned.'

'Well, here I am as you can see, Mr Holman.' She smiled pleasantly at him. 'And how are you keeping? How's that troublesome old back of yours?'

'The lumbago?' He shook his head. 'Frequent murder, Mrs Flight. I don't suppose—'

'Say no more, Mr Holman,' said Phyllis delving deep

7

into her mammoth handbag and taking out a small blue glass bottle. 'A drop before you go to bed each evening should do the trick.' And she whispered confidentially, 'Make it two drops if there's a full moon.'

Mr Holman thanked her profusely, then asked, 'Is it all right for me to be starting up the Flyer now and getting her under way?'

Is it all right? thought Ewan, pretending not to listen. *Doesn't this train run to a timetable?*

Phyllis smiled graciously, extending a gloved hand to touch the driver gently on his arm. 'Drive on, Mr Holman. Drive on.'

Mr Holman turned to go but, in doing so, caught sight of Ewan. He stopped and glared at him.

'That boy annoying you, Mrs Flight?' he asked, in such an obvious way that Ewan squirmed. 'I could have him removed if he is.'

Phyllis laughed dismissively. 'Not in the slightest, Mr Holman. The girls and I won't even notice him there.'

Mr Holman shot a warning look at Ewan, making him squirm again. 'Children are best seen and not heard,' he growled, before returning to his cab, which was joined to, and overlooked by, the rest of the carriage.

Huh! I doubt if an infant school sports day would be heard over this lot, thought Ewan, glancing across at the chattering, laughing, shrieking women; noticing, beneath the table, Phyllis easing off her shoes by the heels and wriggling her stockinged toes, an expression of absolute ecstasy on her face for having done so.

Meanwhile, the Gribbage Flyer had begun its journey. It pulled away from the subterranean platform and left the station behind, emerging into dusty city sunlight—

wheezing and clanking and every last bolt vibrating. Outside, factories and warehouses, wasteland and wire fences went by in a dreary parade. Inside, Ewan found it much more interesting spying on Phyllis and *her girls*.

He soon learnt they had been up to the city for a weekend shopping excursion. They took great delight in opening their carrier-bags to show off their purchases, cooing and trilling at each other—although clearly they must have seen the items many times before. Then Phyllis decided it would be *even more delicious* to play a few hands of gin-rummy—by which time Ewan was able to put names to the other faces around the table nodding their total agreement with her.

Madge, the tall, sensibly dressed one, had grey curly hair and a hooked nose; and beneath her bluff cheerfulness came flashes of something more steely and resolved. Ginnie giggled too much, rolling her eyes; her bright, billowy clothes making an unsuitable contrast with the masses of ginger hair untidily piled up on the top of her head, yet never completely restrained. Bobo was small and mouselike. She wore a headscarf and was in the habit of holding a hand before her mouth whenever she laughed, hiding her teeth which were all of the same size; while her laugh was oddly soundless.

Taking a pack of playing cards from her handbag, Ginnie expertly licked her thumb and dealt. Phyllis won the first game—and the next—and the next. In fact she won every game, her companions applauding each win and shrieking out, 'Oh, well done there, Phyllis.'

Ewan was less impressed. *I don't believe she could win every time—not unless she was cheating*, he thought. Madge seemed to share his opinion. She was looking down at the cards and frowning.

Glancing out of the window, Ewan was surprised to see the train had left every trace of the city behind and was rattling through some flat, rather uninspiring, countryside. Phyllis, growing bored with winning so easily, turned to the newspaper for their horoscopes.

'What are you, Ginnie love?'

'The fish, dear. The fish. Pisces.'

The women's screams of laughter were abruptly cut short on hearing the compartment door slide open. They all turned round expectantly to see a fat woman in a pinafore enter, blowing out her breath and much troubled by a combination of the heat, the train's motion, and the effort it required to manoeuvre a tea-trolley after her.

'You about ready for some refreshments now, Mrs Flight?' she panted.

'My, how scrummy, Mrs Juffkins. Yes, please.' Phyllis glanced around with her moist gleaming eyes. 'What say you, girls?'

'Oh yes!' they cried.

'How pleasant.'

'Super idea, Phyllis.'

Phyllis smiled slyly. 'And what precisely would you care for?'

'Us?' The three other women looked unexpectedly flustered. 'Er . . . but what would *you* care for, Phyllis dear?'

'Umm . . . Let me see . . .' Phyllis made a great show of pretending indecision before coming out with, 'T-e-a, I think.'

'Oh yes, splendid,' said Madge. 'Tea it is.'

'Make mine a cuppa, too,' gushed Ginnie.

'And me,' said Bobo raising a timorous finger.

'Or . . . then again, perhaps I'd prefer coffee.' Phyllis's lipstick formed an innocent smile. Bobo, Madge, and Ginnie stared at each other in horror. 'Do you know,' purred Phyllis, 'I think *I* would prefer coffee.'

'Yes . . . yes, me too,' said Ginnie hurriedly and Bobo was nodding her head as if a nut was loose in her neck.

With a threatening sweetness, Phyllis turned on Madge. 'And what about *our Madge*? What did *she* say she wanted?'

Madge chewed her lips. A strangled sound came from between them.

'What was that, Madge dear?' said Phyllis with a smile that did not quite match the glint in her eye. 'Speak up.'

'*Coffee.*'

Madge brought up the word as if it were a pebble in her throat.

'And there you have it, Mrs Juffkins,' said Phyllis. 'Four of your nice coffees if you would be so kind.'

Ewan was reaching in his pocket for some change when he realized that the tea-trolley was rumbling away from him. Either Mrs Juffkins hadn't seen him or had chosen to ignore him altogether. Phyllis caught his eye and smiled knowingly, her lipstick smudged around the rim of her cup. Beside her, Madge drank with audible gulps, sounding like a drowning woman coming up for air.

If she doesn't like coffee, why is she drinking it? wondered Ewan. He glanced at Bobo and Ginnie sipping nervously, their heads cowered and eyes darting around the table from face to face. Nobody was inclined to be chatty any more. Phyllis dozed—but once Ewan caught an ice-blue eye open and swivel around at *her girls* like a crocodile surveying its stretch of the river, before lazily closing again.

Thirty minutes later the train pulled into Gribbage Holt.

Chapter Two

Ewan quickly decided that Gribbage Holt looked neither interesting nor picturesque, untidily straggling away from the station up a hill to an ugly brick church at the top. He wondered if all the ladies lived locally, as he watched Phyllis rallying her female crew for disembarkation.

'Home, girls!' she cried, as if leading a charge against enemy cannons. Madge went barging up the gangway, her hefty handbag striking Ewan on the head. Yet judging by the withering look she shot him afterwards, she clearly believed *him* the one at fault and herself the aggrieved party.

Ewan hauled at his case, which was as reluctant to get off the train as he was. On the platform the stationmaster stood to attention, medals newly polished on his chest, saluting like a military man as Phyllis's party swept by. Seeing Ewan struggle, however, he sniffed, pushed his hands in his pockets and slouched back to his office, peering at the boy through grubby net curtains as Ewan used the public pay phone to leave word of his safe arrival on his parents' answer machine. It annoyed him that they were out and not hovering anxiously by the phone as he imagined they would be.

'Looks quiet here,' he said accusingly. 'Better go now in case I miss something interesting like a blackbird or a sheep.'

Replacing the hand-set he saw that the platform was

now deserted. With a rattle the Gribbage Flyer crawled off to disturb the peace of some other unsuspecting village. Hot and exhausted, Ewan flung himself down on a bench and closed his eyes.

'You 'im then?' asked a gloomy, unimpressed female voice.

Ewan jumped to his feet.

'I'm Mrs Mulligan, the doctor's 'ousekeeper. I does for 'im.'

Ewan found himself face to face with a small wiry woman who, despite the heat which made the tarmac sticky beneath his feet, wore a belted raincoat and woollen hat. Before he could say anything she picked up his case, the veins in the back of her hand standing out like cables.

'Well, I can't carry a gre't lump like you 'n' all,' she said glumly when he hesitated.

Ewan followed her into the car-park where Phyllis Flight's party was bustling around a gleaming silver Volvo. Naturally Phyllis herself took the driving seat; her stockinged feet stretched out from the car door to cool. Then she slipped on a pair of sensible flat driving shoes, carelessly swinging the red shoes on her fingers.

'Good afternoon, Mrs Mulligan,' she called.

Mrs Mulligan, her eyes grimly fixed ahead, made no acknowledgement. Ewan, trotting behind, wondered if she had heard: then he noticed Phyllis grin and suddenly the car erupted into screams of laughter. For some reason Ewan felt the laughter directed at him too, and the blush behind his ears spread rapidly to his cheeks.

The women were still laughing when they sped by, throwing up a cloud of dust into the faces of the two pedestrians.

'Pah!' spat Mrs Mulligan. It was something Ewan came to admire in her. One of Mrs Mulligan's snorts of disapproval could knock a fly from the air at eight paces.

He squinted up his eyes against the dust, asking innocently, 'Where is *your* car, Mrs Mulligan?'

The housekeeper stopped and stared at him. 'Car,' she uttered. 'What car? Feet good enough for me. Should be good enough for others. Folk always take the easy path these days.' She continued grumbling as she started up the steep hill.

Ewan watched her, her strong determined shoulders hunched. This was not turning out as well as he had hoped. He glanced across to the station shimmering through the rising heat, then back up the lane at Mrs Mulligan.

Perhaps, he thought, *it will be much better once I reach the house and meet Dr Malthus.*

Chapter Three

When the house finally came into view, Ewan had a kind of lumpy, leaden feeling inside, as the last prop of hope was kicked away.

He could not quite believe what he saw.

The house stood alone in a hollow on the far side of the hill with its back firmly turned on the village; its garden was completely overgrown, waist deep in flora of a type possessing either thorns, stings, or vile smelling flowers that even the insects avoided and which later would develop into poisonous berries. The wooden fence leaned out towards the road and the stiff gate testified to the rarity of callers. To be quite sure they remained a rarity, a sign stated bluntly how unwelcome hawkers, canvassers, or visitors without appointments really were.

The house itself, continuing the theme of neglect and decay, was old—but not old and charming. It was built for an age when solidness was the most admired quality in a building. Its walls were thick, allowing only little windows that were deeply recessed. Ivy took the frontage, part colonizing the roof too; and a central chimney, stout enough to moor an airship, cast a shadow over half the garden. The roof was of tile and there were two rows of pointed dormer windows, the higher row so tiny they might have served as doors to a pigeon loft.

Mrs Mulligan caught Ewan's gawp of disbelief and sniffed, twitching her puckered mouth sideways.

'It does for the doctor and it does for me,' she said defensively. 'And don't you go expecting nothin' new-fangled or fancy. It's a good, clean, plain house an' none the worse for that.'

Ewan, still rather stunned from his first sighting, understood this to mean no microwave or dishwasher— or, at a pinch, a telephone. It turned out Mrs Mulligan referred to gas and electricity: water too, unless you counted the hand-pump in the courtyard at the rear.

'I'm sure I'll find it . . . very nice,' said Ewan unconvincingly.

'I 'spects you 'as to.'

Mrs Mulligan led the boy around the side of the house into a kitchen that was cool and gloomy and smelt sourly of cabbage. From its ceiling hung a curl of ancient fly-paper, made curranty with dead insects. A blackened range stood against the chimney breast and beneath the window was a deep square sink, crazed with little black cracks no thicker than a hair. Every worktop was heavily grooved from scrubbing. She nodded curtly at a table covered in plastic gingham.

'Sit yourself there if you're stoppin',' she said, sounding not a bit bothered one way or the other. She removed her coat and hat. 'I suppose bein' a boy you'll be 'ungry?' She spoke the word *boy* as if it were a species of savage animal; and the word *hungry* might have meant some dreadful tropical disease.

Ewan nodded and immediately felt guilty for having done so, so readily.

Mrs Mulligan set some cheese and home-baked bread before him. 'Simple fare for simple folk. Be thankful,' she said, perhaps anticipating criticism; and pushing her head through a clean apron knotted the strings with sharp, quick jerks of her hands.

Ewan sat in silence, cowering over his food, subdued by Mrs Mulligan's efficiency about the kitchen, for no sooner had he done with a knife or plate than it was whisked away from him to be vigorously scrubbed in the sink. Eventually, when he had finished, Ewan found the courage to speak.

'Mrs Mulligan,' he said timorously, 'where is Doctor Malthus?'

Mrs Mulligan sniffed. 'Oh, don't you concern yourself about the doctor. Important man 'e is. Writes papers an' books only the likes with brains can make sense o' up at them you-know-versities. Doesn't 'ave much patience with chil-dren, so you 'ave to amuse yourself as best you can round 'ere.'

'But——' Ewan's courage failed him. Why, he wanted to know, if the doctor disliked children and was so taken-up by his work, had he insisted on Ewan coming to stay with him?

'Now, finish your bread outside,' said Mrs Mulligan shoving him towards the garden.

Ewan lingered at the doorway, loath to enter the poisonous wilderness lurking beyond it.

'Well, go on, I 'as work t' do!'

Ewan shrugged and put all the boredom he felt into the slouch of his walk.

For a while he idly passed the time feeding his crusts to the sparrows then, discovering an ants' nest, watched the steady traffic of insects come and go, placing obstacles in their way. Afterwards he made water gush from the hand-pump and thrashed a path to some ruined outbuildings, but disturbing a wasps' nest there fled back towards the house. Mrs Mulligan's determined face met him through the kitchen window as she grimly scrubbed away at the sink.

Ewan slipped down the side of the house into the front garden, stepping into the shade of the one tree that wasn't stunted, gnarled or a half rotting stump. It was some kind of maple, its elegant leaves as broad as spread hands.

To be fair, it was never Ewan's intention to climb the tree. Not to begin with, at least. First he swung on one of the lower branches and, finding he could hook his heel upon a higher one, pulled himself up and perched there; and since the next branch now came within easy reach, he climbed that too. As he climbed, he parted the leaves to spy on the house, having a clear view into many of its rooms.

On the ground floor the furniture was dark and old; and candles waited on mantelpieces alongside little glass vases containing tapers to light them. More intriguing, however, were the photographs. In every room, upon every wall, Ewan saw framed photographs of the same boy—a boy of roughly his own age—who grinned confidently at the camera. Some photographs were formal sittings, but more often than not they were snapshots of him with his dog or pony, or any number of admiring adults. In some rooms the photographs were trimmed with black ribbon.

Ewan climbed higher. Most of the rooms on the first floor were starkly empty, the wallpaper faded and peeling. Then, noticing the arched window above the porch had curtains, he grew curious, slithering out along a branch to investigate.

Almost immediately he saw that this particular room belonged to a child. A boy. For his toys were set out on the shelves. But the more he peered, the more Ewan had a sense of something that wasn't quite right. Not only were the toys years old, practically museum pieces in some instances, but they were arranged in such a careful way that it was impossible to believe any child ever played with them. Indeed in this respect, the entire room felt wrong; and as Ewan's eyes moved across the neatly made-up bed to the rows of books, their spines perfectly straight, he remembered with sudden fondness his own sock-and-comic-strewn pit at home.

Then Ewan knew what the room reminded him of. It was a shrine.

The moment this thought came to him, he saw there was somebody in the room; and to his utter horror, Ewan realized he had no business to be there spying on him. The man was seated in a dark corner by a small table, a drawn, unhappy looking man. He must have sensed he was being watched, for he suddenly looked up and his eyes met Ewan's. The sadness in them instantly vanished, instead there was fury. He raced across to fling open the window, thrusting out his head.

'What the devil do you think you're playing at, boy? These are private grounds. Get down! Get down at once, I say—before I take a stick to you!'

Such was his rage and Ewan's panic, that the boy lost his grip and fell, his falling body smashing through the lower branches until he struck the ground. At this point Ewan felt entitled to a little mellowing on the part of the man, if not some out-right sympathy—but not a bit; if anything the man became even angrier.

'Young hooligan!' he ranted. 'Take yourself off my property and if ever I catch you here again—'

'But, Doctor Malthus,' cried Ewan, 'I'm Ewan Niles. You asked me here . . . Remember?'

Doctor Malthus remained unmoved. He frowned. 'I don't care who you are or where you come from, if ever I catch you climbing that tree again I'll thrash you to within an inch of your life. Is that perfectly understood?'

Ewan nodded miserably.

The window crashed down and the angry red face disappeared, leaving Ewan still sprawled on the ground.

'I might have broken my leg,' he reflected bitterly. 'Not that anyone round here would care. Nobody would—'

He stopped, his hand touching something cold and smooth under the long rank weeds. Carefully he parted them and peered into the gap. A small metal plaque was secured upon a marble stone. Ewan saw writing and his lips moved as he read.

'I plant this tree in memory of my beloved son, Sigmund, who was cruelly and needlessly taken from me in this life . . .' and there was a date. 'May the tree grow great and strong and never be cut down young as he was. His memory will live on in me for ever.' Underneath was the name *Hugh Malthus*.

'Creepy,' said Ewan to himself. 'The date he died is tomorrow—or rather its anniversary.'

Hearing something that sounded like a giggle, he quickly glanced up. In one of the dormer windows he saw a face. Pale and indistinct. But he recognized it at once.

It was the boy from the photographs.

Chapter Four

Ewan was still feeling queasy about what had happened when Mrs Mulligan shouted him in for dinner (she called it tea).

As a cook, she had not heard of healthy eating, nor did her meal take into account the sweltering heat.

'Good plain food for good plain folk,' she said gruffly, setting a bowl of steaming mutton stew before the boy. Grease spots swam amongst the potatoes and pearl barley; and the tasteless, sticky dumplings, which appeared mercifully small and manageable were, like icebergs, deceptively large, their greater part being concealed below the surface.

As he sweated over each spoonful, Ewan was informed that the doctor didn't enjoy company at meal times, preferring to dine alone.

Huh, thought Ewan. *I don't think Doctor Malthus likes company at any time*; and again he wondered why he had been asked to stay.

Of course he said nothing about the face at the window. He didn't think Mrs Mulligan would make a very understanding listener. Besides, he had buried the sighting under various plausible explanations, chief amongst which was that he had surprised himself with his own reflection. But however much he thought about it, he was never entirely convinced.

Mrs Mulligan, like the doctor, didn't eat with Ewan.

She sat engrossed in the evening paper on the other side of the table, occasionally tutting over the latest murder or scandal. She lit a candle when the shadows began to deepen.

'Mrs Mulligan,' said Ewan.

She looked across at him over her reading glasses, her expression unpromising.

'Mrs Mulligan, how did the doctor's son get killed?'

'Best you don't ask them sort o' questions in this house,' she replied with a flick and a crack of the newspaper.

'But it happened years ago.'

'Might 'ave been yesterday as far as the doctor's concerned.'

'Please tell me.'

With her eyes lowered as though reading she said, ' 'E took a terrible tumble at the front o' the house. 'E 'ad climbed out the window an' they reckon 'e was tryin' to get up on the roof. Always was inclined to be a bit on the wild side was the lad, causing 'is father so much grief 'n' all.'

'And did he fall where that big tree is?' pressed Ewan.

Mrs Mulligan looked up at him in surprise. 'On that very spot. The doctor refused to touch the garden afterwards. An' it used to be bootiful. Could 'ave won silver cups—' Realizing she might have said too much, Mrs Mulligan jumped up and said angrily, 'All this idle talk won't get the pots scrubbed.'

She cleared the table. By the sink was an ancient battery radio, her one and only permitted luxury. She hummed along to some barely audible brass band music, her arms elbow deep in suds. The night was still and stiflingly warm. Through the open door moths were drawn and, swooping too near to the candle, shrivelled and fell like autumn leaves.

Hearing movements overhead, Ewan lifted his eyes to the ceiling.

'The doctor likes to take to his bed early,' explained Mrs Mulligan, drying her hands on a tea-towel. ''E takes to 'is bed early an' gets up early. It sets the routine for the rest o' the house.'

Ewan realized he was getting a strong hint that *he* was expected to go to bed too. He fidgeted in his seat. It was far too hot, and he wasn't the least bit tired.

Mrs Mulligan picked up the candle, its light swirling upon racks of willow-patterned plates. 'I'll show you to your room,' she said leading the way from the kitchen. Ewan followed, hardly able to see much before him, feeling the cold kitchen flagstones soften into hallway rugs beneath his feet.

On the stairs he whispered, 'Mrs Mulligan, why does the doctor have so many photographs of his son?'

Mrs Mulligan stiffened at his impertinence. 'The doctor finds comfort in 'em. There are worse things a man can turn to for comfort.'

Ewan pushed a little further. 'And will he be seeing me tomorrow?'

Mrs Mulligan shrugged. 'The doctor 'e 'as 'is work t' do. 'E doesn't like bein' disturbed unless it's important.'

Ewan was exasperated. 'Why did he ask me to come? I don't understand. It's not as if he can be bothered with me now I'm here.'

''Spects 'e 'ad 'is reasons. Right—' she said changing the subject. 'This'll be your room.'

She opened the door on a small ordinary looking room at the far end of the house. It had no carpet, but the floorboards had been thoroughly scrubbed and, like the rest of the house, smelt strongly of disinfectant. There was a heavy wardrobe with a mirrored door, a dressing-table, a chair, and an iron bed with two mattresses, one stacked on top of the other—so tonight it would really be a case of climbing into bed. A tall window nearly reached to the floor, and through the drawn curtains, Ewan glimpsed the moonlit outline of each window-pane.

He lingered by the chimney-breast to study yet another photograph of the boy who confidently stared back at him, smiling as if amused by what he saw.

Lighting a second candle, Mrs Mulligan pointed out a basin and a jug of water with a slither of soap alongside.

'See that you use it,' she said. 'Dirty boys make for dirty sheets, so I shall know if you don't.'

Ewan continued gazing at the photograph, wondering if she would have spoken to the boy in such disrespectful tones. Somehow he doubted it.

He heard the door click and looking round saw that Mrs Mulligan had gone. Suddenly he felt very lonely, and spotting the familiar battered sides of his suitcase standing at the foot of the bed was like spotting the face of a long-lost friend. Opening it, he took out a writing-pad and pen (favouring purple felt tip, since it seemed to convey more passion and urgency); and sitting down at the dressing-table wrote a letter home—no easy matter by candle-light, his hand casting a shadow across the paper.

The letter drew out all his feelings of homesickness as he described the utter awfulness of Gribbage Holt;

managing to convey the poverty and degradation of his situation in the fact that his bedroom lacked a carpet. He begged for the opportunity to taste his mother's own cooking once more, claiming he would prefer death to grappling with another of Mrs Mulligan's dumplings. As for the doctor, a line of exclamation marks served to suggest what he was unable to put into words. He signed the letter *Your only and ever loving son, Ewan*, before sealing and addressing the envelope.

That should ensure his rescue, he thought, especially if he also telephoned whenever and as often as he could.

He sat back feeling rather pleased with himself for having taken control of the situation. Then, inexplicably, the candle went out and the darkness pounced on him.

There hadn't been a breath of wind in the room and Ewan remained motionless for reasons he didn't understand, but which were quite instinctive. He wondered if the tingling sensation at the base of his neck meant he was afraid. But of what? *This is silly*, he told himself, but still he sat and waited, convinced that this was a beginning and more was to follow. The seconds moved on and his sight grew accustomed to the dark. Around him he saw only what was ordinary and reassuring— walls and furniture and an envelope in his hands glowing powdery blue.

He relaxed, letting go his breath.

In the speckled mirror moonlight glimmered as he crossed to the mantelpiece. Although his eyes were reluctantly drawn to the photograph, he was glad to see the smiling face reduced to a black square in a dark frame. Outside an owl hooted and he jumped.

'Oh, enough!' he said, now angry at himself. He set

the envelope down on the mantelpiece, determined to post it first thing in the morning.

Immediately the letter leapt off onto the floor.

The tingling sensation returned, spreading down his spine. The letter hadn't just fallen, it had flown off as if an invisible hand had picked it up and thrown it.

Outwardly showing all signs of calmness, Ewan picked it up and placed it back on the mantelpiece, this time a little further along.

Again it flew across the room. Ewan flushed with anger, which he directed at the letter itself, as if being defied by a small disobedient animal.

Snatching it up a second time, he slammed it back on the mantelpiece, weighing it down with coins from his pocket.

The letter came alive more determinedly than before, landing by the bed, sending the coins jangling into the grate.

Wildly Ewan spun around, but the room was empty. 'I'm not afraid of you—whoever you are!' he whispered hoarsely, angry because he *was* afraid.

Then he saw something which for the moment his brain was unable to comprehend. The china basin Mrs Mulligan had left for him to wash in was slowly rising up from the dressing-table.

Desperately Ewan dug deep for possible explanations, while with his eyes he followed the basin's progress, as it glided out across the floor and into the reflection of the old mirror.

'Why are you doing this?' cried Ewan to the force that moved it.

He was seized by the unrealness of the situation. Yet

the moment he heard himself speak, reality regained control. The basin dropped under no supernatural power other than gravity, shattering loudly and casting broken fragments across the floor.

Suddenly the door flew open and Doctor Malthus rushed in.

'What happened?' he demanded. 'Tell me everything.'

At first no words would come; Ewan felt as if his throat had closed up. The doctor looked furious at his apparent stupidity.

'An ac-accident,' he finally managed to force out. 'I . . . I dropped the basin.'

'Are you quite sure that was all? Nothing else?' The doctor's words were insistent and probing.

Ewan gave a single nod.

Doctor Malthus seemed to shrink in on himself. 'Go to bed,' he said, his voice cold and unfriendly, and stooping down he picked up the broken pieces of pottery.

When he straightened up again, Ewan said, 'I . . . I'm sorry. I haven't made a very good start here, have I?'

The doctor said, 'It's late, you should be asleep,' and promptly left the room.

Lying still on the creaking bed, Ewan brimmed with far too many thoughts to sleep.

'He didn't believe I broke the basin,' he said aloud to the darkness. 'And yet he almost seemed disappointed when I admitted it *was* me—but who else was there to blame?' Deep down, Ewan wasn't entirely convinced that this was the real reason for his lying.

'The doctor wouldn't have believed the truth,' he suggested to himself. 'Whatever that was.' Yet still this wasn't the true reason.

Ewan thought long and hard about it, until it suddenly grew clear. The main reason he had lied was because neither Mrs Mulligan nor the doctor were being strictly honest with him. That was it. Mrs Mulligan had told him that the doctor always went to bed early—so why was he fully dressed and wearing boots as if he meant to go out or had just come back in?

Why wouldn't someone tell him what was going on?

Then he heard a mocking giggle and sat bolt upright, listening.

The sound stole away up the chimney.

Chapter Five

The following morning, Ewan awoke feeling tired and grouchy. He knew he had been restlessly turning the mystery over and over in his mind, even in his sleep. Staring up at the ceiling, he resolved there and then not to post his letter home until he had found out exactly what was going on.

This decided, he slithered out of bed and gave himself the briefest of washes before throwing on his clothes and going down to breakfast.

A deep silence hovered over the house, more brooding than the previous day's; and on the landing, Ewan was surprised to see a mirror covered with a piece of black satin; while downstairs, vases of fresh flowers stood prominently placed amongst the dead boy's photographs.

'Of course,' Ewan told himself, remembering the plaque by the tree. 'Today is the anniversary of his death.'

In the kitchen, Mrs Mulligan stood solemnly stirring a pan of porridge, stirring in all her woes too, or so it seemed. She wore a black headscarf and did not look round when the door opened and Ewan entered. The porridge was automatically dished up for him a lump at a time, with still no word passing between them. Hopefully Ewan glanced towards the radio—but today it appeared to cower in a corner like a small browbeaten creature that knows when to be quiet.

Deciding to escape to the village as quickly as possible, Ewan gobbled down the porridge—which was quite difficult because it was so salty (he imagined as a consequence of Mrs Mulligan's tears); and he didn't dare ask for any sugar for fear of offending the awful, all-prevailing silence.

Afterwards he fled, running up the path to the lane. The morning was already hot, and finding a stick he rattled it along the fence enjoying the pointless noise of it; then he swished the stick before him at imaginary enemies.

At the top of the hill he stood in the shadow of the ugly brick church, surveying the village spilling down to the station. Nobody was about and Ewan was just beginning to wonder if his escape from the house was merely a retreat into a different kind of boredom, when he caught the sleek black lines of an American limo, its windows mysteriously tinted. It stood parked by a dense hedge and all but blocked the road to any oncoming traffic; behind it was a silver Volvo. The hedge grew out over the two cars and rose up thickly to the height of a house, breached only in one place by a small wooden gate on which rustic letters spelt out the word *Vicarage*.

Pretending to be a detective, Ewan slunk across to examine the limo, carefully working his way around it, before peering through the driver's side window, trying to glimpse the dashboard as if it mattered in solving a crime. He did not realize he was being as closely observed himself until he saw the reflection of the man looming over his shoulder, his watching eyes hidden behind a pair of dark glasses.

Ewan immediately yelped—not with surprise but

pain. The hand now tightly gripping his wrist peeled it away from the vehicle.

'What do you think you're doing, boy?' There was definite menace in the measured words of the question.

'N-nothing much . . . just l-looking,' stammered Ewan. 'That's all.'

The man was not satisfied and his grip tightened. In his long cashmere coat and black leather gloves he had the air of a ghoulish undertaker about him. But even an undertaker would swelter in such heavy clothes as he wore. The man, however, showed no signs of discomfort: his skin was pale, even his lips lacked colour; while his slicked-down hair shone blue-black like the greasy feathers of a crow.

'Pl-please, you're hurting me,' whispered Ewan.

He saw the man smile to himself and nod with satisfaction. His fingers were incredibly strong.

Suddenly the gate in the hedge burst open and Phyllis Flight appeared. She was carrying a heavy glass jar and swayed slightly on her red high heels. Seeing Ewan she gave a small gasp of recognition.

'The boy from the train!' she exclaimed; and the glass jar nearly slipped from her grasp.

Ewan was roughly pushed aside. 'Careful, woman!' the man snarled, snatching the demijohn from her. 'Do you want to drop it?'

Nervously Ewan backed away—then he turned and began running, running as fast as he could. At a safe distance he breathlessly dodged into the hedge, where he was able to watch without being seen. His wrist ached, and as he rubbed it he sensed he had had a lucky escape.

A little further down the lane, the man was opening

the limo's boot, and did not even bother to glance after Ewan. He packed the demijohn inside with extreme care. Ewan glimpsed it only for a second, but in that time he saw it was full of a strange milky liquid—no, he thought afterwards, it was not like a liquid at all, but more like smoke, mysteriously swirling around inside the glass.

'That's the last one,' Phyllis told the man as he closed the boot and locked it.

'I'll still be needing more,' he said.

'More?' Phyllis blinked in disbelief. 'But where, Mr Hendrick? Where?'

'I'll leave that to you to work out, Mrs Flight,' said the man with a cold indifferent smile. He slipped into the car, started the engine and drove away very cautiously, probably because of his cargo.

Phyllis watched him go, frowning to herself. She didn't notice Ewan half shielded by the hedge. But he watched her as she turned and click-clacked through the gateway and up the path to the vicarage.

That night in his room, Ewan lay on top of his bed, head turned towards the dressing-table, watching a lone candle burn. His stare was as intense as a poacher's watching a trap.

He was waiting for the light to be extinguished as on the previous night, but the pear-shaped flame burned steadily down its length, with now and again a flicker or tear of wax.

Ewan yawned and suddenly sat up, his eyes sore for having stared at the flame too long.

'Oh, this is hopeless,' he said crossly. 'Nothing's going to happen.' And he reached towards the candle.

That very instant the flame went out, as if by its own will, and in the darkness Ewan saw a silver thread of rising smoke, the wick glowing red a second or two longer.

Prepared for this moment, he leapt to his feet.

'Whoever . . . or whatever you are,' he whispered, his voice sounding harsh and odd in his ears, 'show yourself now if you dare.'

For a while it seemed as if nothing was going to happen. Then a silver shimmering (Ewan didn't know how else to describe it) appeared in mid air, speedily growing both upwards and downwards to reach the floor.

And he was there.

The boy from the photographs—that confident certainty in his eyes. He flew up, weightless, his features blurring as he sped about the room, illuminating it with a glowing blue light; afterwards coming to rest before Ewan once more.

'Can-you-tell-me-who-you-are?' said Ewan in slow laboured tones, as if addressing a dull-witted child.

The ghost looked amused—yes, definitely amused, thought Ewan. *Good, perhaps it understands me.*

The ghost spoke.

'Don't you know who I am already?' it replied, speaking in a perfectly natural way. 'After all, you spend enough time gazing at me in my photographs.'

'Then it really is you?' gasped Ewan. 'Sigmund, the doctor's son.'

The ghost appeared to wince. 'You know how I hate that name. You only used to call me that when you were sulking and wanted to annoy me. Why don't you call me

Ziggy, like you used to? Or are you in a sulk with me now?' He flew around in a circle before settling again. 'Anyway, I can be in a bigger sulk than you and then I only have to call you Jimbo to make you mad. But I won't. Not if you call me Ziggy. If you call me Ziggy I promise I'll call you Jim.'

'But, Ziggy,' said Ewan astonished, 'Jim Niles is my father. I'm Ewan . . . Ewan Niles.'

Ziggy fluttered a little closer as if to examine him. 'Does your father still sulk?' he asked.

Ewan found himself nodding. 'Yes—except now Mum calls him *James* if she wants to needle him.'

Ziggy thought this was highly amusing and laughed himself backwards. 'But never mind,' he cried, 'at least *you* are here,' and he hovered as if expecting something. 'Well,' he said at last. 'Aren't you going to wish me a Happy Deathday?'

'Happy Deathday?' frowned Ewan. 'What's a *Deathday*?'

It was now the ghost's turn to treat *him* like a dim-witted child. 'Don't you know anything?' he said, folding his arms in irritation. 'That's the trouble with flesh and blood people like you, never a thought for anything that isn't living.' He took a step nearer. 'Haven't you ever considered that, just as there is one day in the year special to you because that's the day you were born, then there's another equally special day, because that's the day you will die. Trouble is, you can never be sure when that day is until it finally happens.'

'But you know yours,' said Ewan.

Ziggy looked at him incredulously. 'Of course I do. I'm a ghost—remember!'

'Er . . . Happy Deathday,' said Ewan self-consciously.

The ghost fell back in a fit of giggles. He performed a perfect backwards somersault in slow motion, landing soundlessly on his feet again. Then lustily he began to sing—

'Happy Deathday to me,
Happy Deathday to me,
Happy Deathday, dear Zig-gy,
Happy Deathday to me!'

Afterwards Ewan joined in with a rollicking version of 'For he's a jolly dead fellow,' and both boys burst out laughing, Ewan collapsing upon the bed, light-headed with excitement and disbelief.

He stared at Ziggy. 'Why did you smash the basin?' he asked.

Ziggy shrugged carelessly. 'Because you refused to believe in me, of course.'

'Ghosts are supposed to do that sort of thing all the time,' said Ewan knowledgeably. 'They make things float—or levitate. Do you do other things too?'

The confident grin shone out once more. 'Oh yes, I do whatever I like,' said Ziggy boastfully. 'Once I made soot fall down the kitchen chimney—turned poor Mrs Mulligan and all her precious pots and pans black.' He laughed. 'But really it was her own fault. She'd been away to visit her sister. I hate being ignored. I hate it more than anything.'

He spoke with such passion that Ewan glanced nervously at the chimney breast. 'You won't do anything like that here? I mean, I'm in enough trouble with your dad as it is.'

Ziggy folded his arms and smiled slyly. 'I might. If ever you ignore me I shall.'

He flew up and hovered about the window like an excited hummingbird, making the curtains spring apart and flooding the room with moonlight.

'Oh, this is a night to be out and haunting!' he cried. 'Come on, Ewan, come with me. We can go haunting together.'

Ewan heard the sash window open to its fullest and saw the curtains billow in. Then he felt an invisible hand grip his wrist.

'Hey!' he cried, suddenly propelled towards the opening. Like a spike of ice a terrible thought ran through him: Ziggy had brought about his own death by falling from a window—perhaps this very one—was he now going to cause another?

The boy's shins struck the low sill. He closed his eyes in terror—ready for that sickening dreamlike sensation when you're helpless to do anything but fall, and go on falling . . .

Chapter Six

But he was flying instead!

Opening his eyes a moment later, Ewan was astonished to see his shadow go rippling across the moon-lit lane below him, his wrist firmly held by Ziggy (although the ghost himself cast no shadow and, to Ewan's intense alarm, the silvery light made him appear even less substantial than before). 'I shan't let go of you,' said Ziggy, adding slyly, 'I could if I wanted to, and you would drop to the ground like a ripe apple.'

'Please be careful!' begged Ewan.

Ziggy's reply was to laugh, his laughter rolling recklessly across a clear, shiny sky.

Ewan found he was shivering. He didn't know if this was from the chill night air (which it was higher up), or from pure excitement. There was simply too much to think about, so in the end he decided not to think about anything at all, merely giving himself up to enjoying the flight. The fields and hedgerows slipped noiselessly by. Presently he said, 'Ziggy, where are you taking me?'

'To meet my friends,' came the reply, and then Ewan saw the church and they began to descend, feeling the air grow warmer as they neared the ground.

St Bartholomew Alone lay at the heart of a village that had died around it hundreds of years before. The fields on all sides were hump-backed with the buried remains of the old community; and from above, Ewan could see the outlines of long-vanished walls and rooms running as shadows in the grass. It was sad to think the only inhabitants now were sheep and even they scattered in panic at the sound of Ziggy's laughter.

The church itself was a semi-ruin, the squat tower half fallen in on itself and sprouting saplings, but the nave was sound; and from the air the leaning grave-stones around it resembled playing-cards set amongst a tangle of bleached grasses and wild flowers.

Ziggy gently set Ewan down on one of the headstones. Ewan swayed unsteadily, feeling the whiskery tufts of dry moss beneath his feet.

Ziggy looked around scowling. 'Where are you?' he cried petulantly. 'Why aren't you here?'

All at once the ground seemed to heave and a white wave of mist burst up, so completely throwing Ewan that he lost balance and began to topple backwards.

'Hey!'

He felt Ziggy catch him, lowering him gradually to the ground. There the boy watched in amazement the white mist dissolve into individual figures, each one a ghost like Ziggy.

'Happy Deathday!' they cried together.

Ziggy flew up, literally glowing with pleasure. 'I shall burst!' he cried. 'Like a shooting star. *Pow! Pah! Boom!*'

As he raced back and forth across the sky, Ewan crept away and found a flat, table-like tomb so he could sit and observe.

He was flabbergasted to see how numerous the ghosts were: admittedly some more distinct than others, who were little better than puffs of mist (Ewan supposed them to be the very ancient ones). However, it was really no different to watching any gathering of living folk—old and young together. *But then*, thought Ewan, *the very idea of age is turned on its head once you die, for it is possible for a ghost child to be older in actual years than another ghost who is fully grown-up*. It was a peculiar thought as the ghosts cavorted.

'Pray, would it offend you greatly, sir, if I were to sit myself alongside you?' asked a rather grand voice just then. And Ewan found himself replying 'Not at all' to a ghost dressed in ruff and hose, and carrying his own head beneath his arm. But by this stage Ewan's astonishment could be stretched no further and he was quite prepared to accept whatever next came his way—even a headless ghost.

The ghost settled himself, resting his head neatly in his lap with his arms folded upon it, as if it were no more than a parcel.

'Oh, pray excuse my lapse,' he said, suddenly picking up his head again and rotating it towards Ewan. 'Sir Edward Upton, your obedient servant, sir.' And as his head returned to his lap, he added wistfully, 'Pray do refrain from remarking upon Ed being an unfortunate name for one such in my predicament. The jest is a poor one that wears exceedingly thin after four hundred years. Very thin indeed, sir.'

Ewan agreed he wouldn't and shyly introduced himself. 'Er . . . Sir Edward, may I ask you a question?'

'No doubt, Master Niles, you wish to learn something of the circumstances in which my head parted company from the rest of me.' The knight sighed.

'Does it upset you to talk about it?'

'Not in the least, sir,' replied Sir Edward, his head

swivelling around on its chin to face the boy. 'But when my dancing of the galliard brought me renown and open admiration across three counties, I find being distinguished by a mere artless trifle disagreeable in the extreme.'

'Well,' said Ewan politely, 'it is quite . . . well, eye-catching.'

'Beheading,' said the ghost simply, blinking ahead. 'The old chop-chop. Or rather, in my instance, just chop. You see, Master Niles, I paid my executioner the handsome sum of five shillings and sixpence to make neat work of it. Methinks he did too.' He spoke as if discussing the cut of his cloak instead of that of his neck. His headless shoulders shrugged. ' 'Tis no more than the price you pay for earning a queen's displeasure.'

'And tell me,' whispered Ewan. 'What is it like to be a ghost?'

Sir Edward sighed wearily. ' 'Tis as grey a way of existing as my beard used to be,' he said. 'No hunting, no feasting, and . . .' (Here his voice sounded particularly sorrowful.) 'no dancing. A ghost comes into being, Master Niles, whenever a natural life is violently cut short; and we remain a prisoner here in this world of the living until the day we are released.'

Before Ewan was able to question him further, a rush of silver went streaking by like a comet, its shiny tail remaining afterwards in the sky.

'Come on,' a familiar voice badgered in his ear. 'Today's my Deathday. I won't have another for a whole year. Let's do something exciting.'

'When you can claim to have existed for as long as I have,' said Sir Edward mournfully from his lap, 'you

41

are less mindful of individual years and pay greater heed to the passing of centuries.'

Ziggy circled the church leaving a glittering halo around its tower. 'Everyone has to play hide and seek,' he announced forcibly.

'But, Ziggy, we know all the places to hide,' protested the veiled lady in white. 'You tend to discover them after the first two hundred years.'

Ziggy laughed carelessly. 'But my new friend Ewan Niles doesn't. It's perfect, he won't have a clue *where* to look.'

Ewan suddenly sensed himself becoming the centre of all ghostly interest, with even Sir Edward lifting his head to examine him anew.

Ziggy landed noiselessly behind and, putting his hands over Ewan's eyes, said, 'Count slowly to fifty—then come and seek us out.'

He soared up like a rocket, and the other ghosts swooped away too in a rustle of excited whispers. Soon all that was left were their shiny interwoven trails—like snail tracks—fading slowly in their wake.

'Don't make it too difficult for me!' Ewan cried after them, and covering his eyes, slowly began to count. 'One . . . Two . . .'

Reaching fifty he sprang up and gazed about him. Already the moon was on the wane, its light thin and grey—although the broken tower loomed up impressively, no less black and cliff-like than before. In the stillness, dry hollow-stemmed grasses rattled and sighed.

Ewan stroked his arms realizing, as if for the first time, that he was alone in the middle of the night, stranded in a haunted graveyard. His first instinct was to turn and flee. But why? What was there to be afraid of? Gradually his panic subsided and his heart stopped thudding in his chest. More calmly he made his way to the church door, set back in the blackness of its porch. At first, when he took the handle, he thought the door locked. But it was simply its great weight. Putting his shoulder to it, the door creaked open like timber splitting.

'Ziggy,' he whispered into the dark nave, the whisper scratching around the stonework before returning to him.

As the darkness grew less intense before his eyes, Ewan saw the church had been cleared of all its pews, but at the eastern end a canopied pulpit remained, and there was also a font, grit glinting as sharply in its roughly hewn sides as in a mill-stone. The windows arched into high blunt points, with traceries like skyward-reaching branches hung with diamond-shaped panes of opaque yellow glass, little ancient bubbles trapped within them.

Then he caught sight of a nose and set of whiskers so distinctive, he confidently hurried across the empty church towards them.

'Sir Edward,' he whispered.

His outstretched hand touched cold stone, finest Purbeck marble in fact. And he saw what he had stumbled upon was the knight's effigy, carved in his living likeness, with his head firmly joined to the rest of him: while the frilled ruff about his throat seemed mainly there in defiance of the queen's executioner. His long elegant fingers met in prayer upon his breastplate and below his square-toed shoes lay an obedient dog or lion, its ears broken off and its face worn to an expression of endearing good humour.

As he stood gazing down at the effigy, Ewan heard the door unexpectedly creak open again. Turning his head, he was just in time to see it swing to, the noise of its closing amplified by the church's hollowness.

For some reason he felt uneasy.

'Who's there?'

He waited for a response and when none came his sense of unease grew. Stealthily he crossed to the southern aisle, where the shadows were more complete and the air noticeably colder, rising through the flag-stones from the crypt below.

He shivered then abruptly checked his breath as the darkness stirred and a ripple of cold air touched his bare arms.

'Who's there?' he whispered in a small frightened voice. 'Who is it?'

In reply something lunged towards him. Ewan tried to step back but to his utter horror found he couldn't—his shoulder was firmly held.

But it was not the cold melting touch of a ghost.

It was something altogether more human.

Chapter Seven

'My, my, what have we here, squirming and squealing?' said an irritated female voice.

A torch was lit and flashed in Ewan's eyes, preventing him from seeing anything beyond grey outlines.

'It's that boy again,' uttered a second female voice, quivering with indignation.

Although Ewan was unable to see them, he quickly recognized the two women by their voices. The first voice belonged to Phyllis Flight, the second to Madge; and it was Madge's powerful hand which tightly squeezed his shoulder.

'Let me go!' he cried, struggling.

'Not until you have spilled the beans and told us exactly what it is you are doing here,' growled Madge, sounding more like an arresting police officer.

The prospect of trying to explain anything about that night made Ewan struggle all the more. 'Let me go!' he cried again, his echoing voice taunting him from around the church.

He didn't hear the door swing open, but suddenly two more torch beams flashed through the darkness. Ginnie and Bobo came flying in.

'Phyl-lis! Phyl-lis!' gulped Ginnie breathlessly. '*He* has come.'

Phyllis let out a piercing shriek which had the effect of stunning Ewan into silence and putting an end to his struggles. Meekly he allowed himself to be hauled outside. There, the women's torch beams crossed another, a solitary light coming from the opposite side of the graveyard. The beams resembled lances drawn up to do battle.

'Mrs Flight!' roared a man's voice. 'I challenge you to tell me the exact nature of your business here at this hour.'

'In a churchyard, Doctor Malthus?' threw back Phyllis sarcastically. 'Where else do you expect to find a vicar's wife? Besides, I could ask the same question of you, or this boy here. He is, I understand, a guest of yours.'

She paused, savouring the triumph of her retort. Dutifully Bobo, Madge, and Ginnie shone their torches on Ewan, who shrank miserably beneath the bright accusing glare.

A brief—possibly puzzled—silence ensued from the other side of the graveyard, before the doctor cleared his throat and said in rather more subdued tones, 'The boy is with me, I admit. Come here, boy, and don't wander off like that again. It might be *dangerous*.'

Ewan swung his gaze up at the women, scowling defiantly.

'What shall we do? What shall we do?' gushed Ginnie nervously.

'Interfering little brat,' said Madge, giving Ewan a shove.

'Oh . . . let him go,' said Phyllis. 'The boy is nothing to us.'

'Go!' cried the three other women in dismay.

'I'm waiting, boy!' called the doctor again, this time more sharply.

Phyllis smiled her lipstick smile and patted Ewan on the head as if he were a three year old. 'Yes, dear, run along now, do what the good doctor says.' Then muttered to her companions, 'Come, girls. Away. We must put this unfortunate episode behind us.'

They swept out of the churchyard in a cloud of indignant self-righteousness, noses in the air as they passed the doctor. With more uncertainty Ewan made his way around the gravestones, delicately stepping upon the doctor's light as if it were a fragile carpet. When near enough the boy said fiercely, 'My name is *Ewan* in case you've forgotten.'

Doctor Malthus said nothing, he was more concerned to see the women go. Only when their torches were well into the distance did he speak, and then it was with a curt 'Come on', and they silently followed after them, along a footpath, across open fields.

The moon was much lower now and the ragged hedgerows seemed like the old night's fraying edge. From beneath their feet the smell of warm earth was released, mingling with the slightly cabbagey reek of vegetation.

As they went, Ewan suddenly felt a prod in his side and sniggered involuntarily. The doctor flashed his torch-light at him as if he were some kind of lunatic, but Ewan managed to blink back at him straight faced. It had been Ziggy, Ewan realized at once; just as he now sensed Ziggy's presence right there beside him, sometimes catching hold of his shirt as he clambered over a stile or brushing his face with a leaf.

The journey home turned into a long one by foot—a long way in silence too. Behind the far trees, Ewan saw the women's torches flicker and was almost envious when their laughter came floating back to him through the stillness.

He glanced sideways at the doctor. *Why doesn't he speak?* he wondered. *Why doesn't he ask me what I was doing at the church?*

Reaching the village, Doctor Malthus lingered at his gateway, watching intently the other lights continue up the hill. When they disappeared behind the dense hedge at the vicarage, he clicked off his own torch and led the way into the house.

In the darkness he turned purposefully and Ewan heard him say, 'Go to your room, boy, and this time be sure you stay there.'

Ewan pushed past him, but on the stairs he paused.

'Ewan—take great care,' said the doctor softly. 'You are more headstrong than your father was. Don't let it lead you into trouble.'

Ewan ran up the rest of the stairs and into his room. The curtains billowed out in welcome. As he was kicking off his shoes he heard a familiar giggle.

'You're fun, Ewan Niles,' whispered a voice. 'I'm so glad I'm haunting you.'

Chapter Eight

Ewan awoke late the following morning, feeling cool air trickling across his brow, and opening his eyes the first thing he saw was the curtains swelling like sails at the open window.

He remembered the previous night, all at once and vividly. There was never any question of 'Did it really happen?' or 'Was it a dream?' Ewan was a boy strong in his convictions and beliefs.

He got up and washed and dressed then went downstairs, noticing that yesterday's roses had spilled a scattering of petals. He was just thinking that cut flowers were necessarily also dead flowers, when suddenly he jumped back in surprise, his mouth gaping stupidly.

Ziggy's photograph had just winked an eye at him.

Ewan gave an airy, nervous laugh before scurrying on to the kitchen, where he had a second surprise. Doctor Malthus was there, awkwardly hovering at the end of the table, his unexpected presence perturbing poor Mrs Mulligan, who kept folding and unfolding a tea-towel. She was relieved to see Ewan, for now she was able to take out her discomfort on someone.

'There you are,' she said at once, hurrying forward and fussing him to the table. 'Porridge is nearly set 'ard—I hopes you washed properly. Them nails look as if a good scrub wun't go amiss and that 'air's never set eyes on a comb . . .'

49

Doctor Malthus smiled blandly at him; and Ewan kept throwing him curious glances down the length of the table, fully expecting the doctor to launch into a strict lecture concerning his adventure last night. But not a word about it was mentioned; oddly, it was as if the boy had arrived at the house that very morning, for the doctor kept harping on about his journey down here; then when this was about exhausted, he turned to the health and welfare of Ewan's family, and afterwards reached the inevitable topic of the weather and the unrelenting heatwave and growing drought. Mrs Mulligan scrubbed heavily and meaningfully in the background and slowly it dawned on Ewan that both of them knew all about Ziggy's ghost, yet a conspiracy of avoidance existed on the subject. It was simply never spoken of.

Apart from a stilted 'Yes' or 'No', Ewan said very little, getting down to the serious business of tackling Mrs Mulligan's porridge. Then he snorted back a giggle. Upon the wall behind the doctor's head, the hands of the old pendulum clock were beginning to spin. Only Ewan was in a position to see them, spinning ever faster until they had become a total blur; while below the clock face, the pendulum swayed more and more erratically, as if meaning to throw itself right across the kitchen. Ziggy's doing—Ewan hadn't the slightest doubt; and in an effort to sandbag the laughter threatening to explode out of him, he packed his mouth with porridge, then started to choke.

Mrs Mulligan promptly marched over to pound his back. 'Some folks 'ave eyes bigger than their bellies,' she said reproachfully.

Hardly had Ewan swallowed down the porridge and regained his self-control, than he saw something that started him off all over again.

The pepper-pot had grown weightless and was slowly rising up off the table.

This time nobody could fail to notice—and Mrs Mulligan, artfully snatching it out of mid-air, slammed it back down in its rightful place.

'Of course, you may find us a little quiet at Gribbage Holt at first . . .' the doctor was droning on, completely unfazed.

Mrs Mulligan cast her eyes down the entire table length, defying anything else on it to move. Ewan covered his mouth with a hand, his suppressed giggles having turned into a bad case of the hiccups.

'*Hic!*'

A spoon began to levitate. Mrs Mulligan took a wild grab at it. The spoon playfully jerked from her reach and her bosom knocked a milk bottle flying. Calmly the doctor lifted his cup and saucer, allowing the white spill to trickle beneath them.

'*Hic!*'

Ewan's hiccups grew worse the more he wanted to laugh but fought against it. His eyes brimmed with water, and his shoulders shook violently.

Like a cat mesmerized by the bird it stalks, Mrs Mulligan was blind to everything except flying cutlery. A fork dared to rise, followed by another spoon. Bad temperedly, Mrs Mulligan barged around the table making ever more desperate pounces on various pieces of silverware, occasionally catching something, but more often bumping against

51

the table itself—spilling milk or coffee and rattling the china.

Pretending to be oblivious to all around him, Doctor Malthus went prattling on about nothing of consequence. Not that Ewan was paying the slightest attention.

'*Hic!*'

Every time he jerked with a hiccup, porridge flicked from his spoon onto the plastic gingham. That made him want to laugh even more and, as he desperately battled against it, he wondered why he was playing this *nothing is happening game* along with the others.

Suddenly Mrs Mulligan shrieked. She rounded upon invisible air, crying, 'Do that again an' I'll—'

A fork now darted angrily in her direction, waspish in its movements, its three stings to the fore. Mrs Mulligan drew back in alarm.

Her exaggerated look of horror was too comic for Ewan to bear. Blurting out an apology of sorts he dashed from the kitchen, falling to the ground outside, his stomach hurting from half stifled laughter and hiccups, and undigested porridge; and he laughed wildly and uncontrollably until *that* hurt even more.

From then on, Ewan's time was taken over by Ziggy and the ghost world. He learned how to become a night person, sleeping throughout much of the day and joining Ziggy at moonrise. But even when dozing, Ziggy came to him invisibly, nipping him awake, desiring to be entertained, not left alone—like a spoilt child who always demands attention.

The most surprising part to Ewan was how readily this

arrangement was accepted by the rest of the household. If he slept through a meal time nobody woke him; and Mrs Mulligan got into the habit of preparing and leaving out cold dinners for him. Likewise, at night, when Ziggy went roaring through the darkened house, laughing madly and slamming doors—this was all perfectly tolerated, for the doctor and his housekeeper couldn't have avoided hearing the noise. Indeed, if it didn't waken them, it certainly prevented them from going to sleep.

It remained a great mystery to Ewan, who often wondered why it was so.

Chapter Nine

On Sunday morning Ewan stumbled sleepily into the kitchen for what some would call breakfast, but what he now considered supper, since his intention was to go straight to bed afterwards. In the kitchen Mrs Mulligan was sitting solemnly at the table, hands crossed before her, one resting on the wrist of the other, and wearing a narrow-brimmed felt hat in place of her workaday knitted one. Bluntly she told him to make his own breakfast. She never cooked or baked on a Sunday—it was part of her beliefs. Her chapel was very primitive; its congregation both firm in its certainties and strong in its disapprovals. She would ask him to accompany her there this morning—but children were one of the things disapproved of.

'Is that the brick church up on the hill?' asked Ewan innocently.

Mrs Mulligan drew in her breath, offended, twitching her mouth to one side. 'I'll not step one foot inside that place,' she said tartly. 'Not into a church where the minister don't recognize good nor bad.' She gave one of her famous snorts. ''Ow can he,' she said, 'with that wife o' 'is carryin' on as she does? Now stop wastin' m'time with idle tittle-tattle, you'll make me late for chapel an' that's somethin' else the brethren frown upon.'

Ewan cut a chunk of bread and cheese and watched her go. As did, so it happened, someone else a little

54

further up the lane. It was Ginnie stationed in a phone box, trying to squeeze herself down out of sight, but always popping up again like a champagne cork. Her breathless excitement made her flushed and the telephone receiver was like a living fish in her hands.

'Oh, Phyllis, it's so divine being a spy,' she trilled. 'Yes, yes, she's gone . . . What's that dear?—Speak up . . . Oh yes, quite sure. The coast is perfectly clear.' She laughed delightedly. 'Er . . . tell me, dear, is it now I have to say Roger and out?'

The knock at the door fifteen minutes later was timorous, almost scratching; and when Ewan opened it he at first saw only the tall imposing figure of the Reverend Irvin Flight, standing with his eyes raised to heaven. Thinking him in prayer and not wanting to disturb him, Ewan waited patiently in silence.

'Fine Edwardian porch, this,' said Reverend Flight gazing down at the boy. 'A pet interest of mine—architecture.'

He half turned, closing his fluttering eyelids—a habit of his when either speaking or nervous. 'There *is* someone home, dear,' he called and his wife, Phyllis, slunk from behind to take her place at his side, almost before he had finished speaking. Her lipstick extended a fiery greeting and she wobbled slightly on cherry red heels.

Reverend Flight said, 'My wife bade me call before the ten o'clock service.'

'Shall I fetch Doctor Malthus?' asked Ewan dubiously. 'He's working in his study right now.'

For a second, Phyllis's eyes narrowed and became cat-like. 'Oh no, no,' she cried. 'I'm sure he doesn't want disturbing. Besides it's *you* we came to see.'

'*Me?*' said Ewan surprised.

'My mind simply would not rest,' declared Phyllis, slipping past the boy and into the house before he could invite or prevent her. 'That dreadful misunderstanding between us the other night has been preying on me, I could not bear for you to go on thinking badly of me and my girls. So then, thinks I, I know, I'll call in and explain everything to the dear young man in person.'

'My name is Ewan,' said the boy coolly. 'Although it seems no one round here wants to use it.'

They were, all three of them, in the living room by now, the room Mrs Mulligan insisted on calling the best parlour. Reverend Flight came in more hesitantly, wiping his feet longer than was necessary and running a hand through his hair which was thick and silver. 'Fine chimney piece,' he said, unable to prevent himself.

'*Irvin,*' said Phyllis, flashing him a reproachful look above her spectacles. 'We are not here to discuss your dusty old architecture, we are here to make clear muddy waters.' She sat herself down in the best armchair, legs crossed, casually swinging a shoe by her toes. Not at all like most vicars' wives, considered Ewan, sitting on a stool on the opposite side of the rug.

'You see, it's like this, Edwin—'

'*Ewan.*'

'Ewan,' she smiled sweetly. 'There have been so many attacks on local churches of late by vandals and thieves and suchlike, that my girls and I have organized ourselves into a little vigilante group. Naturally, when we caught you up at St Bartholomew's, we quite innocently mistook you for one of those particular ruffians. It was an easy conclusion to draw.'

'Ah, St Bartholomew's,' murmured Reverend Flight. 'Rather imposing twelfth-century doorway.'

'Oh, Irvin,' spoke his wife irritably. 'Do be quiet.'

'Yes, dear,' he replied, fluttering his eyelids.

'Anyway, Eustace,' she continued to the boy. 'I sincerely hope we did not hurt or frighten you at all, I . . . would never forgive myself if we had.'

She put on such an expression of self-loathing that her husband moved across and gently squeezed her shoulder.

Phyllis sniffed and hauled her great handbag on to her knees, from it taking a glass jar of green crystals. 'Medication,' she smiled palely at Ewan. 'I hope you don't object, but I find when I become emotional it goes straight to my sinuses.'

'She's a martyr to her sinuses,' confirmed her husband.

Phyllis carefully unscrewed the jar. Ewan watched, fully expecting her to breathe in its beneficial vapours and was surprised when she started wafting the jar about the room, spreading the crystals' sickly sweet smell. As she waved it, she muttered inaudibly under her breath; and for some inexplicable reason Ziggy's anguished face flashed into Ewan's mind. Reverend Flight sat smiling, his hands spread on his knees. But Ewan felt uncomfortable, wishing more than anything for them both to be gone.

Abruptly he leapt up. 'Are you sure you wouldn't rather speak to Doctor Malthus?' he asked.

'Oh no, no, no,' said Reverend Flight, dismayed at the very prospect. 'I'm afraid the good doctor tends to misunderstand the worthwhile work dear Phyllis performs in the community.' He fluttered his eyelids. 'I don't think it at all wise to send for him.'

Ewan suddenly felt numb. The smell from the jar was overpoweringly strong and so sweet it set his teeth on edge. He gazed at Phyllis and saw her expression was strangely hard, possessed, so to speak, by determination. Ewan thought he would be sick if he smelt the crystals a moment longer.

'I'll make a pot of tea,' he gasped, trying not to inhale; and he sprang to the door without waiting for a response.

In the kitchen, Ewan propped himself against the table. He felt weak and befuddled; and before his eyes the kettle turned into such an unfamiliar object that it might have come from Mars. He picked it up and it seemed heavy and awkward to handle. He had just finished filling it in the yard, the fresh air bringing him back to his senses, when he heard an awful commotion arising from the front of the house. Dropping the kettle he dashed back into the kitchen and spied on the hallway through the gap between the door and its frame. He saw Doctor Malthus, his back to him and shoulders risen in fury.

'Get out of my house!' he was roaring. 'Get out of my house now—before I fling the pair of you out with my bare hands!'

Reverend Flight emerged from the living room looking pale and shaken. Phyllis came right behind; her expression a mixture of annoyance and sly triumph.

'Come, dear,' said the vicar taking his wife by the arm. 'Let us leave this place with dignity.'

Doctor Malthus pointedly stood aside to let them pass. 'And never show your faces around here again—d'you hear!' he bellowed up the garden after them before slamming the door.

Ewan watched the doctor double up against the door as if in pain. Then he suddenly straightened. 'Ziggy,' he whispered—and then he was running up the stairs shouting it.

'Ziggy! Ziggy!' His feet thundered as if meaning to bring the whole house down around him.

At the top of the building, Ewan heard his voice break out into an anguished wail.

'She has taken him from me!'

Chapter Ten

Ewan spent a long anxious while waiting in the lane. Behind him the house was quiet now. But it was an uneasy kind of quiet. Ewan wrung his hands and every few minutes stepped out into the road, glancing up it for the returning figure of Mrs Mulligan. In the end he heard her before he saw her.

> 'All people that on earth do dwell:
> Sing to the Lord with cheerful voice—'

When she marched around the bend and saw Ewan, she halted and thoughtfully regarded him, chewing round her lips as if meaning to spit. Then she approached and said quietly, 'She's been 'ere, 'asn't she?'

Ewan nodded, his voice thickening when he spoke. 'And it's all my fault. But I didn't mean it to happen.'

She put her hand firmly on his shoulder and steered him towards the kitchen. He didn't like being back in the house: everything in it seemed to silently accuse him. Pulling out a chair, Mrs Mulligan guided him round, sitting him down as if he was totally incapable of the simplest action. Then, as businesslike as ever, she removed her hat and coat, put on her apron, found the kettle outside, refilled it and placed it on the range.

The brewing pot was set on the table between them.

'I did 'ave words with the doctor about it,' began Mrs Mulligan. 'I told 'im straight 'e should tell you everythin'' t'begin with. But 'e insisted 'e knew best, so I kept m'peace.' She worked her shoulders round. ''E said the less you knew the better. An' see what a fine mess 'as come o' it now.'

She poured the tea, strong and sweet.

Ewan closely watched her movements as if they were significant. 'I understand about Ziggy,' he said slowly. 'The doctor's son. We all knew about his ghost, didn't we?'

Mrs Mulligan gave a single stiff nod. 'That were one o' the problems. The doctor thought 'e might scare you off if 'e told you 'ow matters stood. Thought it best you discovered gradual for yourself.'

'And Mrs Flight?'

Mrs Mulligan's reply came back with customary directness. 'A witch.'

Ewan shot her a glance across the table, half expecting a wink or smile to follow, but he should have known Mrs Mulligan was never one for flippant remarks.

'They all are,' she continued. ''Er an' them cronies she 'as about 'er an' calls 'em *er girls*.' She scoffed. 'An' 'er a vicar's wife 'n' all. No wonder the Church o' England is in the state it is. But then all o' 'em are respectable on the face o' it. There's Madge Block, wife o' a bank manager, with 'im as little as she is big; and Ginnie Flowers: married to a school master—teaches *art*. Then there's that mousy 'un as calls 'erself Bobo an' follows everywhere like a labrador: a county librarian. 'Ad the nerve to fine me for bein' overdue last week, would you believe?'

'And you're telling me they're all witches?' cried Ewan.

Mrs Mulligan nodded and, following her usual practice, tipped her tea from cup to saucer and took a slurp from it.

'Pillars o' the commoonity,' she sneered. 'Or ought to be. But too much time on their 'ands 'as led 'em astray. That's the curse o' the washin' machine an' other time-savin' de-vices. Time was you scrubbed by 'and for hours on end an' at nights fell into bed exhausted. They think it a bit o' a lark to dabble in witchcraft. They don't know what they do. Them's muddy waters that they paddle in,' she added darkly.

'But I still don't understand,' said Ewan. 'What has any of this to do with Ziggy's ghost?'

Mrs Mulligan sniffed. 'For some time them *so-called* ladies 'as been stealin' ghosts. Kidnappin' 'em, if you can call it that, what with their poor bones lying six foot under in the ground. An' the doctor 'as been tryin' 'is 'ardest to stop 'em.'

'But why should anyone steal ghosts?'

'Ghosts is power. Like 'lectricity. A witch can do much with that. But, mark me, somethin' much darker lies behind what Phyllis Flight does. Somethin' t'do with Cumberforth Hall. That big old 'ouse—though these days it goes by the name o' Ghostlands. It's one o' them whatyoucall'ems—*theme parks*.' She rolled her lips. 'They're strongly disapproved o' by the chapel brethren.'

Suddenly Ewan understood something. 'So the doctor sent for me because my dad and Ziggy had once been friends, and he hoped Ziggy and me would be friends too; that way we'd be together and I'd protect him from the witches.'

'The doctor knew 'e couldn't be with 'is son all the

time,' said Mrs Mulligan. 'An' them witches were watchin' an' ready t'pounce the moment 'is guard was down.'

'Then it's all my fault,' said Ewan miserably. 'Instead of protecting Ziggy I end up being the one responsible for his capture.'

'You let 'er into the 'ouse,' said Mrs Mulligan, seeing no reason to lessen his burden of guilt. 'You invite a witch across your threshold an' you're askin' for trouble.' She sniffed and rose. 'Now I best go see 'ow Doctor Malthus is. I 'spects 'e'll be broken. Loved 'is son 'e did, even beyond the grave.'

'I'll come too,' said Ewan clambering to his feet. Mrs Mulligan shook her head and pushed him back down.

'Best you don't,' she said. At the door she paused. 'Oh, an' I meant t'say, I posted that letter o' yorn.'

'What letter?' asked Ewan distractedly.

'The one you 'ad gatherin' dust on your mantel. I mean, it's only right an' proper you should send word 'ome t'your folk. I posted it yist'day while delivering me "Evils o' Pleasure" leaflets about the village.'

With these words she left him staring at the closed door in utter dismay.

Oh no, he thought. *When Mum and Dad get my letter they'll be down here like a shot—I'll be whisked away before I can even start to put things right again.*

He wondered if it was worth telephoning home from the village phone box, and he imagined his conversation running along the lines of, 'Guess what, Mum and Dad, you're going to receive this letter and—ha-ha—I don't want you to believe a single word of what I've written . . .'

That might work on his father, but his mother was far too suspicious.

His eyes focused on the calendar hanging on the back of the door. He calculated that if the letter arrived on Monday, this left him the rest of that day and part of the next in which to do something.

Suddenly he leapt up; he dashed out into the garden, down the path and into the lane. With only a couple of short breaks, he didn't stop running until he sighted the half ruined tower of St Bartholomew Alone.

Outwardly the church appeared little different in daylight than it did by night. The gravestones around it stood dappled with sunshine and splashes of yellow lichen; and at intervals there arose a grasshopper's wistful chirrup. Standing as it did so far from any road, there was nobody to be seen, and Ewan passed through the lychgate and into the church, his footsteps echoing in the cool emptiness. Slowly he gazed about. In the corners of the pointed windows ancient cobwebs had woven themselves into a white fur, and on the ledges dry crusty jam jars held the petal-less stems of dead flowers. The effigy of Sir Edward Upton reclined in faded glory as before, his long fingers forming a steeple upon his chest.

Then Ewan stopped dead—confused at first as to which of his senses had alerted him. Hesitantly he sniffed the air, then again with more urgency; and catching the smell stronger the second time, was left in no doubt. It was the sickly sweet smell of the green crystals; and he realized the witches had returned and done their work.

He went straight across to the knight's tomb.

'Sir Edward!' he hissed. 'Sir Edward, if you are still

there and can hear me, please, please make yourself appear.'

His words sent a shiver through the air and he saw goosebumps break out at his elbow and spread down his arm: around him the church turned as cold as a cave in winter.

Only when he was on the point of giving up did a mournful voice finally answer.

'Who speaks to summon Sir Edward Upton?'

'It's me, Sir Edward,' cried Ewan. 'Ziggy's friend. You remember? *Ewan Niles*. Please, won't you make yourself visible to me?'

Slowly, like a melancholy sun, the head of Sir Edward rose from the stone chest of his own effigy. Ewan waited for the body to appear after it. When it didn't, Sir Edward stared sadly at the boy, saying, 'What you see, Master Niles, is all that remains to me. A man who once danced the prettiest galliard on the handsomest legs in three counties.'

Ewan perched himself on a corner of the tomb. 'Tell me what happened,' he said.

The knight's head bobbed a little higher as if in anger, then depression made it sink back down. 'Oh, Master Niles, 'tis pitiful. Last night those . . . those hags and harpies swept through the churchyard, spreading enchantment like great spiders their webs. We were but poor helpless things before it, as one by one the strong magic did first ensnare and then enslave us. In this way they . . . they took possession of my lower regions; but my brains, living in my top half, had wit enough to outflank them. I told my arm to cast my head as far as 'twas able, and by good fortune it came to rest a goodly

65

way outside the church boundary, beyond reach of their witchcraft. Ah, but the shame of being so reduced. 'Tis more than a body can bear.'

'They took Ziggy too,' admitted Ewan grimly.

The floating head tutted. 'There exists no respect for the dead these days. We are but dust, swept beneath the carpet.'

Ewan tactfully agreed. 'Why are the ghosts being rounded up, Sir Edward?' he asked. 'Mrs Mulligan reckons something much darker lies behind it all.'

Sir Edward tried to nod in agreement, lost balance, fell over his chin and dropped into Ewan's lap. Ewan was less startled than once he would have been. The knight gazed up at him forlornly. 'The poltergeist has arisen,' he whispered.

'But I've heard of poltergeists,' said Ewan. 'Aren't they ghosts the same as you?'

The outraged head flew up at once. 'Most certainly they are not. Why a poltergeist is pure malice— unforgiving of all things living. It would rather destroy that which it cannot enjoy, and only want of power prevents it from doing so.'

'But don't you see?' cried Ewan. 'If it is the force rounding up the ghosts it might take its power from them—is it possible?'

'Aye, Master Niles, more than so.'

A gloomy silence settled upon them until Ewan said, 'Tell me, Sir Edward, what sort of things can a poltergeist do?'

'It can perform all manner of calamities,' replied the knight unhappily. 'It can create itself master of the elements, calling forth hurricanes and floods. It can bake fields till the crops shrivel, or can set a mountainside sliding. It can bring disease, or stir malcontent, or draw vermin from every part of the compass. It feeds on the misery of others, even of its own kind—my poor ghostly brethren.'

'Then we must stop it!' cried Ewan, leaping up. 'Sir Edward, do you know the whereabouts of Cumberforth Hall?'

'*Do I know?*' exclaimed Sir Edward. 'Why of course I know, 'tis my old country seat, from such a time as I possessed two seats, one upon the land, the other upon my legs. Handsome legs. Did I tell you, Master Niles, I used to dance the finest g—'

'Yes, yes,' said Ewan. 'Quickly, we must get going there.'

' 'Twas ever the way of the living,' sighed Sir Edward to himself. 'Always making such great haste.'

Chapter Eleven

Together they flew up from the churchyard.

Flying with Sir Edward was even more nerve-racking than flying with Ziggy, if only for the fact there was less of him and soon even that disappeared! Ewan grabbed the invisible head firmly between his hands.

'Pray, sir,' gasped the knight, 'don't squeeze so.'

'I can't help it,' replied the boy. 'I wouldn't be quite so nervous if I were at least able to see you.'

Patiently Sir Edward explained that ghosts were always invisible in bright sunlight. It was simply not their element. Unless, of course, they were that most powerful of all ghosts—the poltergeist.

They flew on, Sir Edward remarkably agile and speedy for a bodyless head, and Ewan said as much.

'Methinks a favourable headwind blows to our advantage,' commented the knight, who was then puzzled by Ewan's laughter.

Soon Ewan's arms began to ache, and he shut his eyes to prevent himself getting dizzy from the height. He imagined his style of flying—with his arms outstretched before him and feet trailing loosely behind—to resemble closely that of a gravity defying dive. Far less the Flying Dutchman and considerably more the Flying Goalkeeper.

Meanwhile, the land flashed under them. Mile upon mile of scorched pasture dotted with scrubby bushes wilting in the hot breeze; and it occurred to Ewan that this heatwave might possibly be the poltergeist's work and it gave him some indication of its power.

'Fear not,' he heard Sir Edward say. 'We are almost there.' Five minutes later he was set down on the brow of a hill and, surprised at finding his legs so wobbly, immediately sank to the ground. Sir Edward invisibly nuzzled close.

'Is that Cumberforth Hall?' asked Ewan.

'Aye,' replied the voice at his side.

Down below them in a valley, Ewan saw a rambling country house, its centre rising up in an impressive jumble of pepperpot turrets and candystick chimneys. Yet, despite its grandeur, Ewan also saw that parts of it were little more than an empty shell, noting the free-standing gables, and windows that were blank and glassless.

Sir Edward sighed deeply and Ewan was unsure whether this was at the sight of his former home, or for what had sprung up in place of the once beautiful grounds, whose planting the knight himself had supervised. Instead of the old knot gardens and clipped yew walks, there had appeared various noisy rides and gaudy side-shows; and behind the house, where the kitchen gardens had provided food throughout the year, a dusty building site now stood, expanding the funfair still further. *Phase two* this was called: Ewan read it on a fence billboard.

As to the rides themselves, these all carried a super-natural theme. One of the largest was a kind of roller-coaster, its little cars resembling skulls; and when the cars were really speeding, they burst into a haunted house only to re-appear from it further down and in a different direction. Judging by the queues, this was one of the park's most popular attractions. Over it sailed a bloated ghost balloon with *WELCOME TO GHOST-LANDS* emblazoned across it in scary, shaky letters.

'As if all ghosts were nothing so much as a plain winding-sheet held aloft by a breath of wind,' growled Sir Edward in disgust.

Ewan was about to agree, when suddenly he was aware of another figure on the hill-top with them. Hurriedly he shushed the knight quiet, and turning saw that the stranger was Reverend Flight, who approached with an unsure smile.

Poor man, thought Ewan. *It's not his fault his wife is a witch*; and he deliberately gave him an extravagantly cheery greeting. The vicar was mildly taken-aback by this.

'Hello again—Ewan, isn't it?' he said, at the same time casting a quick, cautious glance around. 'Er, anybody with you?'

Ewan knew he referred to Doctor Malthus, so he grinned and shook his head.

Reverend Flight visibly relaxed. He closed his eyes and breathed in deeply. 'Like to drive out here and take a regular turn,' he admitted. 'Helps blow away the cobwebs between services. And such an interesting building too, don't you think?' He nodded down at the Hall. 'Tudor mostly—dating back to the time of Sir Edward Upton.'

Ewan hugged his knees, smiling to himself. 'Do you know much about Sir Edward Upton?' he asked mischievously.

'Oh no, no—nothing much at all. My area is

architecture. Though I do know he was a bit of a rogue—no better than a bandit really—cheating the royal treasury out of—Ow! I declare, something's bitten me. Must have been an insect.'

Ewan, hastily changing the subject, said he wished *he* was as knowledgeable about old buildings.

Taking this for encouragement, Reverend Flight fluttered his eyelids and smiled. Sitting beside the boy he took it upon himself to point out various features of architectural interest, although Ewan only half listened. He was more absorbed with the sinister little skull-cars which were cranking up the steep incline, before racing away at breakneck speed, down the twisting track and through the haunted house with its crooked doors and crooked windows and crooked, crooked walls.

His attention was quickly reeled back, however, when he heard the vicar say, 'Cumberforth Hall is supposed to be the most haunted house in all Britain.'

'Is it?' said Ewan, turning to him.

Gratified by the boy's enthusiastic response, Reverend Flight continued, 'Well, *it was* until destroyed by a mysterious fire during the last war. Some claim the fire to be the work of a poltergeist.'

Ewan thoughtfully plucked at a piece of grass. 'Do you believe in those sorts of things?' he asked. 'You know— ghosts, poltergeists . . . witches?'

'Good heavens, no.' The vicar closed his eyes and laughed briefly, then abruptly grew solemn. 'Some days it is difficult enough simply to maintain one's faith. But no . . . no. Take it from me, Ewan, there are no such things as ghosts—Ow! . . . Do you know, I think that blessed insect has bitten me again.'

Ewan quickly clambered to his feet and self-consciously offered the man his hand. 'Thank you. I have to go now,' he said.

Reverend Flight looked disappointed. 'Must you? So soon?'

'Yes. It's been extremely interesting talking to you.'

'Has it?' The vicar looked genuinely surprised.

'Bye!' called Ewan already running away, allowing himself to be drawn down the steep gradient of the valley, gathering more and more speed as he went, until he found he was running because he was unable to do otherwise. Below him stretched a dirt track road, and he knew his legs would not stop until they had carried him straight over it and run themselves to a standstill.

The big black limo with darkened windows came bumping along the track, throwing up a thick cloud of dust. It blared out a warning—no intention of stopping. Ewan was on a direct path to collide with it and still his legs pounded like pistons.

Then, when it appeared as if an accident was unavoidable, something yanked hard on the boy's collar (Sir Edward, of course, gripping with his teeth) reining him to a halt so abruptly that his feet flew up and he hit the ground, violently rolling over and over in the dust.

Dazed, but unhurt, he had just time to glimpse the limo disappear past a gate marked 'Private—Strictly no Public Admittance.'

'That's the one,' he heard Sir Edward whisper in a fearful voice. 'That's the poltergeist.'

Ewan said stupidly, 'But that's Mr Hendrick.'

Chapter Twelve

Sir Edward was unable to go any further with the boy.

' 'Tis the ring of iron,' he whispered apologetically. 'Ghosts may not pass over it.'

Ewan squinted up his eyes and glanced across the road. 'You mean the gate and fence?' he said, adding, 'Is that how Mr Hendrick stops the ghosts from escaping once they are brought here?'

'I fear 'tis so.'

Ewan strode out into the dirt track road. 'Wait here for me,' he said.

He felt a gentle nudge in his back. 'What is your intention, Master Niles?'

Ewan shrugged irritably. 'How do I know? I hope to think of something once I get inside.'

'Pray, if you chance upon my body,' Sir Edward called after him, 'be good enough to remember me to me with kindness.'

Ewan tagged on to the end of the queue filing into the theme park through the main gateway, which was flanked by two stone pillars. On top of each pillar was a ferocious dog, sitting up on its haunches and clutching a mossy shield between savagely clawed forepaws. A small boy asked his mother what the shields were and was told they were the family arms.

'Arms?' scoffed the father, glancing up at the statues.

'Those brutes look bloodthirsty enough for it to be the postman's legs.'

Ewan paid his entrance fee and was swung inside by the turnstile. At first he went with the flow of the crowd, not knowing what else to do, yet bit by bit was drawn to the roller-coaster, with the restless little skull-cars clattering around the tortuous circuit.

Just then two giggling girls came off the ride, one clutching her chest, the other disentangling her long hair with her fingers.

'Brilliant that,' shrieked the first. 'I screamed m'self stupid.'

'I know, I heard you,' said the second, rolling her eyes.

'Them special effects in the haunted house were great,' continued the first excitedly. 'If ghosts were real that's just how you'd expect them to look. Dead good.'

Hearing her words strangely quickened Ewan's steps. He joined the queue for the ride. Amongst so many, his was the only unsmiling face. Fretfully he drew in the dust with the toe of his shoe. The line shuffled forwards, cars left and returned again, usually with their occupants flushed and giggling. Then, at long last, it was Ewan's turn. He had a car to himself. A man winked at him as he brought down the protective barrier over Ewan's head and locked it into place. Once he was secured inside, the car jerked into motion and Ewan was thrown back against his seat by the sheer steepness of the incline. Before him was open blue sky, the land having completely vanished from sight.

Up and up cranked the car. It seemed to go much higher than when viewed from the ground.

He slumped forwards when the car levelled out at the

top; then his shoulders struck the protective barrier and suddenly he found himself staring at the ground—thundering towards it, as if by some terrible accident he had broken free of the track and was plummeting over the edge. Unsure whether to be terrified or thrilled, Ewan's grip tightened; and remained tight as he was tossed left and right through a rapid succession of corkscrew bends.

A jolting drop. Suddenly the haunted house loomed straight ahead. Ewan gasped, seeing no way of avoiding smashing into its crooked roof. At the very last second, the track dipped sharply. An entranceway. Hardly had Ewan registered it there than its doors crashed open. Darkness swallowed him. Skull eyes flashed on like headlights. A siren wailed!

First, a cobwebby attic. Ghosts springing from chests, screaming from rafters. A bedroom. Crooked pictures and a fourposter bed. Ghosts ambushing him from beneath the quilt—diving through the wall. Reappearing in the bathroom. Bursting up from the toilet and vanishing down the sink. Dining room. Ghosts about a table, turning, grinning, raising their goblets in a gruesome toast. Kitchen. Pots and pans flying—hurled by feuding ghosts. Cellar. Ghosts swooping down—wave upon wave like attacking bats. And then smashing out into sunshine again. Braking. Slowing. Stopping at the point of departure.

'What's up? Look like you've seen a ghost,' joked the man releasing Ewan's safety barrier—speaking the remark as if he didn't say it at least a hundred times a day.

Ewan made no reply. He couldn't. He climbed out of

the car and made his way down the steps. He walked so slowly people bumped into him.

Had he really seen what he thought he had?

He tried to remember again . . . In the cellar. The ghosts forced to perform like circus clowns. Yes, he was sure now.

It had been Ziggy.

Chapter Thirteen

Ewan sat on an empty bench beneath dusty trees gloomily staring at his hands. He wondered what to do next. The most obvious thing, of course, was a second spin on the ride to try to make contact with Ziggy. But really that was hopeless. A waste of time and effort. He idly watched a skull-car descend from the top of the incline and carry its screaming passengers through the haunted house. It took no more than a few seconds. And the electronic wails and groans from inside— amplified to the point of distortion—would drown out any other voice, no matter how loudly raised.

So he sat staring at his hands a little longer, paying scant attention to the endless stream of happy people trailing by, the little kids in their pointed witch hats or grinning at him with plastic Dracula fangs. Nearby, a small building with windows like coffin-lids and doors inscribed like gravestones did a brisk trade in blood-burgers, Frankensteinfurters, knickerbocker-gories and spooka-cola. And you couldn't ask for chips: no, you had to play along with the menu, ordering coffin-nails which came all bloody in tomato sauce. The smell of fried onions made Ewan feel sick. The theme park was so cheap and tacky and noisy that no real ghost would ever choose to make it his home.

By late afternoon the heat was less fierce and the crowds had thinned enough to expose the litter on the tarmacked open spaces. A public address speaker crackled into life and a voice like that of a crabby witch announced, 'This is Evil Vera letting you know that Ghostlands closes in fifteen minutes. Be sure to take all your belongings with you; and folks, that includes young children, or I shall take great pleasure in eating them for my supper. Heeeeeehahaha!'

It was the word *belongings* that lodged in Ewan's mind. He repeated it to himself a few times with growing excitement.

'That's it!' he cried, jumping up and startling a passing family.

Straight away he raced back to the skull ride. A handful of people stood waiting there now, anxious to squeeze in one more go before home-time.

'Excuse me . . . excuse me.'

The man who had cracked the feeble joke earlier on glanced across suspiciously. 'Sorry, mate, waste of time you queuing: this ride finishes for the night after these last few.'

'No. You don't understand. I don't want a ride. I've . . . er . . . lost my watch. I think it came off in the haunted house. My dad'll kill me if I don't find it. Can I take a look?'

The man lowered the safety bar on the final ride of the day; he pushed a button and the car set off.

'Can't let you in there on your own. Orders from the boss. Nobody's allowed in there, not even me.'

'Please! My dad'll hit the roof if I don't at least try to find it—'

'Okay. Okay.' The man shot a sly glance around. 'I'll just make sure the power's shut down, then we'll take a quick look—and I mean quick. And you better not let on to anyone you've been inside—okay?'

Ewan grinned with relief. 'I promise,' he said. 'Thanks.'

The last ride came squealing home. The boy and his girlfriend got off, she all jelly-legged and hanging on to his arm more than was strictly necessary. The ride-man shoved the car into a siding behind the others, forming a row of skulls; then he threw a large lever. Immediately the generator's hum murmured away into silence.

'Come on, quickly,' said the man.

Ewan scurried over the rails to the far side. Ducking under the raised track he followed the man to the haunted house. Half concealed at its base was a small hatch on which was painted: 'Absolutely no unauthorized personnel'. The man tipped back his baseball cap with a screwdriver he'd flipped from a top pocket.

'Good job I can't read,' he winked.

He removed the screws in less than a minute, leaning the hatch-door against the wall.

'I'll go first,' he said.

Crawling after him, Ewan found himself in the haunted dining room. The man had a torch and shone it around. Ewan really didn't expect to see any ghosts, he knew they would be far too wary. He blinked at the furniture which was made disproportionately large and was crooked and garishly painted—except where nobody saw, and there it was unfinished and shoddy.

'How can anyone be scared of this stuff?' sneered the man.

'I think it was in the cellar part.'

'Eh?'

'The cellar. That's where my watch came off.'

The man sighed. 'Come on then, we'd better go see.'

A set of discreetly hidden service steps led down to the cellar. The metal treads rang beneath them.

'You look over there, while I look over here,' Ewan told the man.

'You'll need my torch, won't you?' he said.

'No, the watch is luminous. I'll see it glow.'

The man shrugged and moved away, sweeping his torch before him. No sooner was he out of earshot than Ewan whispered, 'Ziggy? Ziggy? Can you hear me?'

He waited a long time before a response. Then someone—or thing—plucked his shirt sleeve.

'Ziggy?'

A faint shimmering cloud about the size of his spread hand gradually appeared. Nose, eyes, mouth. The eyes were closed; and altogether the features were as indistinct as a face trapped beneath the ice of a frozen river.

The sight so shocked Ewan he drew in his breath.

'What's that?' called the man. 'You found it?'

'Uh? No . . . No. Not yet,' returned the boy, trying to control the wayward tone of his voice; and turning back he saw the ghost mouthing something at him. Ewan moved his lips in time with Ziggy's and found himself saying, 'Help me! Help me!' over and over as the ghost's face dissolved away like a snow-flake.

When next the man spoke Ewan jumped, because without the boy noticing he had come up right behind. 'I don't think it's here,' he said. 'You'll have to tell your dad it was lost somewhere else. Sorry.'

'No, it's okay,' replied Ewan indifferently. 'Thanks for helping me look.'

Crawling back over his steps, Ewan emerged into daylight, covered in theatrical cobwebs. He paused in brushing himself down, conscious of a security camera high on a metal pole, the lens tilted towards him. He jerked his head round. A second security camera also angled his way.

Then Ewan saw him.

Mr Hendrick.

Dark and sinister upon the steps of the Hall.

He pointed a finger and, as if struck by a physical blow, the boy staggered back, reeling from the full intensity of the poltergeist's hatred.

The next moment Ewan was running—running as fast as he could, head down, but vaguely aware of a ring of security guards closing in around him. He tore through the main gateway, with only the briefest glance up at the two savage dogs keeping guard there.

'Master Niles! Master Niles! May I be so bold as to offer you my services?'

'Quickly, Sir Edward, get me away from here!' shouted Ewan.

Sir Edward understood his urgency and, gripping Ewan's collar in his teeth, lifted him off the ground.

Scudding up the valley's side, Ewan felt the poltergeist's power reaching out after him. Cold fingers raked his back trying to claw him down.

'Faster!' he urged.

Sir Edward heard and flew a zigzagged course until, with distance, the poltergeist's grasp suddenly slackened and slid away, clutching at air.

Buoyed up like a cork, Ewan and Sir Edward rose to the top of the hill and, passing over its brow, flew on in relative safety.

Chapter Fourteen

After a dispirited parting at St Bartholomew's, Ewan left Sir Edward and struck off alone across the parched fields towards Doctor Malthus's house. However, the moment his hand touched the gate, he wheeled away from it and strode purposefully up the hill towards the ugly brick church at the top—or more precisely, perhaps, the vicarage next door.

The bushes made a formidable wall, protecting the house from prying eyes: and the wooden gate seemed, in Ewan's mind, to offer too exposed a way of entering. Hearing female voices rising from the garden, he forced a way through the hedge and found himself in a shrubbery, crawling along the dry, stony ground until a clear view of the lawn presented itself, all the way from the french windows at the rear of the house to the rose beds on the opposite side. Phyllis and her followers were basking in the last warm rays of the afternoon.

'Are we having a delicious time together, or what, girls?' Ewan heard Phyllis coo; and he saw Ginnie and Bobo nod wildly (Madge just the once).

Except for Madge, the other women wore long, loose, flowery gowns, the print on Ginnie's and Bobo's exactly the same. Phyllis's straw hat had an elegant wavy brim and was adorned with real roses as shockingly red as her lipstick. Madge folded her arms. *She* wore knee-length khaki shorts and a cardigan. Like a cat, Phyllis stretched herself out upon a sun-lounger. The other women sat around her, upright on canvas chairs.

Phyllis shifted slightly, sighing decorously. 'Today,' she announced, 'I shall be Héloïse, Queen of all the Belgians.'

'You were that last week,' said Madge gruffly.

'Ah,' smiled Phyllis with a hint of steel. 'How like *our Madge* to remember.'

'I would very much like to be Anne, Baroness Windermere,' spoke up Bobo in a sudden rush of words, blushing furiously afterwards. She waved her hands as if cancelling everything out. 'I mean, Harold and I often take our holidays there. It would be so pleasant to have some sort of association.'

'Something far away and romantic for me.' (Now it was Ginnie's turn.) 'How about the Countess Isabelle-Maria from Argentina, known to her devoted admirers as the Lady of the Pampas.'

'Hmm, it has a certain ring to it,' agreed Phyllis. She half turned. 'And how about *our Madge*?'

Madge's jaw firmed as she thought. 'Hmph, I've a fancy for a touch of foreign m'self . . . Griselda . . . Griselda, Princess of the Urals—female-warrior and defender of her people's liberty.'

Phyllis peered critically over her spectacles. '*Female warrior*, dear? Do you think that quite plausible in support stockings? Besides, I see you more in the way of a dowager duchess myself.'

Madge scowled, but before the argument could develop further, Ginnie and Bobo immediately leapt in, flapping like a pair of pigeons, and prevented it. 'Can we start now, Phyllis dear?' pleaded Bobo. 'Oh, I'm so excited!'

Phyllis smiled, and reaching under the sun-lounger trawled out her cavernous handbag. From it she took a large glass jar. The three other women drew back, making disgusted noises and faces on seeing the toad inside; and the toad, equally unhappy for seeing them, desperately slithered up the glass, only to slide back down again.

Coy and knowing, Phyllis carried the jar to the middle of the lawn. She walked barefoot, and in her other hand Ewan saw a twig stripped of its bark.

'Do take great care, Phyllis sweet,' called Ginnie.

'Oh yes, dear—be very careful,' chimed in Bobo.

Concealed by the shrubbery, Ewan watched Phyllis place the imprisoned toad on the ground and circle around it, speaking all the time in a strange unfamiliar language that was full of harsh growls and unexpected clicks; and every now and again she bent down, touching the top of the jar with the twig while making signs in the air with her free hand.

Suddenly there arose the sound of glass splitting and a column of sweet smelling purple smoke billowed up from where the jar had stood. Ginnie clutched Bobo—both watching enthralled the smoke clear towards the rose garden. And there, in place of the toad, now stood something that might have been human, had it not betrayed its true origins by the warts upon the backs of its hands, its wide mouth, bulbous eyes, and extra-large feet, splayed at an angle a ballet dancer would weep to see. It wore the livery of an old-fashioned footman: ruffles at the throat and buckles on its shoes.

The watching women broke out into spontaneous and

85

rapturous applause. Even Madge managed a grudging, 'Bravo there, Phyllis!'

'Mistress,' bowed the toad-servant, unable to disguise a slight croak in its voice. 'I 'ere to serve you. Okey-dokey, lady?'

'Yes. Bring my guests champagne and you be sure it is the finest: as you see we are four noble ladies, used only to the most delicious that life can offer.' Phyllis spoke with the dismissive tones she imagined all titled ladies used on their servants. She re-joined her friends, draping herself languidly across the sun-lounger.

After a moment's hesitation the toad-servant went away, returning with a tray of glasses and a large bottle of champagne. It amused Ewan to see the creature struggle against a natural inclination to hop, the crystal glasses chiming alarmingly against one another; and when it clumsily uncorked the bottle, the *pop!* so startled the poor thing that Ewan half expected it to dive straight into the shrubbery alongside him.

Meanwhile, the ladies had taken out their fans, seeking their cue to flutter from the vicar's wife, with Madge adding one or two extra flourishes of her own.

The toad-servant brought around the champagne, but only Ewan saw it make an expert snatch at a fly, swallowing it down in a noisy gulp. *Yuk—disgusting*, he thought.

Prodding her creation with a folded fan, Phyllis said imperiously, 'My man, I believe a package for me has just been delivered.'

The toad-servant blinked its wide eyes at her.

'Over there on the table!' she whispered, gesturing irritably.

'You want I go get?'

'Just fetch it!' glared Phyllis.

The package was brought over on a silver salver and Phyllis greedily snatched it up.

'Why, dear ladies,' she declared in a trembling, breathless voice. 'Its sender is the King of Macedonia. Hearing word of my beauty he sends tribute.'

The news set Ginnie and Bobo bubbling excitedly. All Madge said after a deep slug of champagne was, 'Didn't he send you something last week, dear?'

'Look, *pearls*,' glowed Phyllis pantomiming surprise as she scooped up the necklace and slipped it around her throat.

'Oh . . . nice,' murmured Madge. 'Yet more pearls. Do you think the King of Whatyoucallit bulk buys for discount? Or does he just happen to like oysters?'

Phyllis shot her a venomous stare and seemed on the point of coming to equally venomous words, when her expression abruptly changed—the colour draining from her face, making her lips appear more luridly red than ever. Around her, the faces of the other witches mirrored her expression—a mixture of disbelief and unease.

'M-Mr Hendrick, how pleasant.' All her former confidence vanished, Phyllis stepped forward to greet her visitor; leaving Ewan to wonder how he managed to appear like that. No car was heard to pull up in the lane, and Mr Hendrick certainly hadn't come in by the garden path, since Ewan would have spotted him straight away. One moment he wasn't there—the next he was, like a menacing shadow, his very presence curdling an otherwise idyllic summer's evening.

Slowly he turned his head, his gaze more terrifying for

being unseen, hidden behind the familiar dark glasses. 'Is this how you fritter away the power I give you?' he hissed. 'On frivolous nothings?'

He clapped his gloved hands together, the sound like a shot from a pistol. The toad-servant immediately shrank back into a common pond variety, desperately belly-flopping across the lawn. The champagne and crystal glasses were replaced by an old milk bottle and jam jars and Phyllis gave a feeble cry on seeing her pearls revert to rotting crab-apples on a hairy string. She threw them to the ground with a shudder.

'It's nothing more than a game,' she said nervously. 'A harmless diversion with a few dear friends.'

'*Diversion!*' Mr Hendrick spat the word back at her. 'If you want a *diversion* bring me that boy who was hanging round my car—the one you caught up at St Bartholomew's church the other night.'

'Er . . . certainly, Mr Hendrick. Is it for any particular reason?'

'Because I tell you,' said Mr Hendrick nastily. He paced up and down on the grass. 'That boy—I feel uneasy about what he may know already. The surveillance cameras caught him this afternoon poking about at my place, but he slipped away before I could get him. I want him brought to me and sooner rather than later. Understand?'

'Certainly, Mr Hendrick. The girls and I will get on to it straight away.'

When Phyllis had led Mr Hendrick away, the three other women let out their breath. Bobo fanned herself rapidly as if bringing herself round from a near faint.

'How he troubles me, that man,' she whispered. 'And so unbelievably rude too.'

The other two nodded in agreement.

'I often wonder if it's worth it,' said Madge carelessly. 'I mean, a few supernatural powers but we still have to be at that fellow's beck and call.'

'Shhh,' hissed Ginnie. 'Here comes Phyllis. Poor lamb looks quite shaken.'

'I take it she's abdicated from the Belgian throne for the time being,' said Madge loudly.

'Hush now,' said Bobo. 'Don't be unkind.'

Phyllis smiled like an invalid at their consoling expressions. Then with a breath she gathered up all her strength.

'Bother!' she cried.

Ginnie and Bobo ran forward, making a fuss of her. 'I suppose we'd better go and find that brat,' said the vicar's wife uncharitably.

Deep in the shrubbery, Ewan had already decided the time was right to retreat and was painfully hauling himself over the pointed stones. The toad hopped past his face like a showman from a circus, flaunting the ease with which it could be done. At the boundary hedge, the boy paused, peered up and down the lane and, seeing it empty, slipped from the garden. That same moment, the witches flew through the gateway.

'There he goes! There he goes!' squealed Ginnie.

'Tallyho!' boomed Madge.

And the hunt was on.

Under normal circumstances Ewan would have left the four women standing—Phyllis especially, as she tottered on her heels, wincing at bunions and painfully nipped toes. But Madge, pushing back her sleeves said, 'Leave this one to me, girls,' and, arching her arm, catapulted her handbag through the air. It struck Ewan on the back, knocking him off balance and sending him sprawling in the road.

The next thing he knew four female faces were staring down at him.

'I hope you haven't hurt him, Madge,' said Bobo with touching concern.

Madge snorted. 'Nonsense. Stout made boy like that should be able to bounce back from a few biffs and knocks.'

She snatched up her handbag and from it produced a pair of handcuffs. 'Always carry a spare set—never can be too sure what lies around the next corner,' she explained, snapping one bracelet on Ewan's wrist, the other on Phyllis's.

'Oh, how marvellous,' cooed Bobo. 'Just like detectives on the television.'

Ginnie went scuttling down the lane to fetch the car, which appeared a couple of minutes later with Ginnie peering short-sightedly over the steering wheel.

'Huh!' sneered Ewan. 'I would have thought broomsticks more in *your* line.'

Phyllis regarded him with moist blue eyes. 'Don't be silly, dear,' she said. 'The Volvo has power steering and heated seats.'

Chapter Fifteen

Ewan sat slumped in the rear seat, boxed in between
Phyllis and Madge, who blocked out his views to each
side. Every time he scratched or drew the back of his
hand across his nose, which he did more than he strictly
required, he chose the hand manacled to Phyllis,
dragging *her* hand along with his.

Pointedly she said, 'Boys have such re-volting habits.'

'Keep still, fidget,' growled Madge at her most formidable and prison-warderly; and Ewan sat glowering
ahead, watching Bobo thrashing about in the front
passenger seat like a bucking bronco rider. Ginnie may
have been short-sighted and too vain to wear spectacles,
yet she drove as if auditioning for a police chase, accel-
erating into corners in the fond belief that tyres were
supposed to screech in order to prove they were still there.

Nobody criticized her; amongst the group it was
considered bad manners to find fault with another lady's
driving. Bobo tittered nervously and Phyllis kept
touching her top lip with the very tip of her tongue as if
probing her lipstick to find out whether it remained
intact.

Presently a gate flanked by two stone dogs was picked
up by the car's headlights (for the twilight had advanced
into darkness). Beneath one dog a camera swivelled, and
Ewan swore its lens focused like a human eye—then the
gate electronically rolled open.

Ginnie brought the car to a halt on the gravel before the big house, in front of a sign reading: 'Phase Three: Reconstruction of Cumberforth Hall—the most Haunted House in Britain'; and the passengers alighted, the women smoothing the creases from their clothes and straightening their hair—Ginnie's falling out of place almost immediately.

'Madge, love,' smiled Phyllis. 'The key, if you would be so good.' She motioned to the wrist with the handcuff clamped to it.

Madge made a great show of rifling through her handbag, pulling out such things as you'd never expect a bank manager's wife to have need of. Why, the tools alone would have done an enterprising burglar proud; while other, more mysterious, objects were obviously connected with magic. As she rummaged, Ewan thought he glimpsed a self-satisfied smile on her face, so he wasn't the least bit surprised when she calmly announced, 'Phyllis, dear, I've just remembered. There *is* no key.'

Whereupon the atmosphere turned more poisonous than that of a cave of cobras holding a spitting competition. But also, at that moment, the main door of the Hall opened and a sinister figure stood in a slither of bright light. The women shrank back a little.

'So you've done something right for once,' called Mr Hendrick, spotting Ewan and coming down a few steps towards them.

'Ah yes—but we have one slight *tiny* hitch, Mr Hendrick,' gushed Phyllis, her struggles to release herself growing ever more frantic. Rounding on Madge she screamed, 'Do something, Madge dear!'

But Madge only shrugged.

'We can try greasing your wrist with butter, dear,' suggested Bobo, always full of practical household hints, adding less helpfully, 'But we don't have any.'

Mr Hendrick looked on with undisguised contempt.

'I don't know why I waste my time on you,' he snarled. 'You other women clear out!' He smiled grimly. 'Mrs Flight will have to follow on later—when she has figured a way out of her present predicament.'

The three women scurried back to the car, scattered as if by his breath; Madge, elbowing Ginnie out of the way, seized the driving seat. Doors slammed, the engine roared and the car sped away churning up gravel. Phyllis watched it go feeling hurt and betrayed, her mouth dropping open in an unuttered exclamation.

'Bring him inside,' said Mr Hendrick.

He led the way into the Hall, whose interior was quite unpredictable, for one room might be dark and empty and open to the stars, while the next was just as likely to be enclosed and furnished and brightly lit with candles. Ewan felt Phyllis trembling. 'I shall miss Evensong,' she said. 'Irvin will worry so.' Yet that was not the reason she trembled.

'In here,' ordered Mr Hendrick, opening a low door into a storeroom, which still smelt of charred wood from the great fire: the stonework pink and scorched over a high window.

'Mr Hendrick, I feel I must protest,' said Phyllis weakly. 'Can I not appeal to your better nature?'

He laughed in her face.

Ewan was angry. 'Of course you can't!' he cried. 'Don't you see it yet? He has no better nature. He's not human—he's a poltergeist!'

'You don't know what you say, dear,' said Phyllis dismissively.

Mr Hendrick smiled. 'I was right. You have found out more than is good for you, boy. I see I shall have to take steps to protect myself.'

'What do you mean?' cried Phyllis all flustered. 'Really, Mr Hendrick, I must protest.'

Ewan tried to peer through the dark glasses into the poltergeist's eyes, but couldn't. What did he intend to do? he wondered. An 'accident' perhaps—something on one of the rides arranged to look like mechanical failure . . . For a second the image of the skull-cars flashed into the boy's mind—had he caught the idea from the poltergeist?

He shook his head to clear it, but the thought stuck. *And what then . . . ? And what then . . . ?* it forced him to consider, until finally the answer came. His own ghost would become another valuable addition to the growing army of slave ghosts—and a little more power to fuel further acts of malignity, which the poltergeist could feast off like a vulture.

'I think you have gone too far this time, Mr Hendrick,' cried Phyllis, who still did not seem to fully understand that the theme park was merely a convenient cover. 'I refuse to be a ghost gatherer for you or your dismal funfair a moment longer. I am the wife of the vicar of Gribbage Holt and a valued member of the parish council, I insist—'

The door slammed on her indignation. They heard the key turn on its opposite side.

'Despicable little man,' hissed Phyllis darkly.

Ewan sighed. 'How many more times? He's *not* a man.'

'Quite so, dear. Hold still a moment.'

Ewan felt his manacled hand manipulated like a puppet's. Phyllis was rummaging in her handbag. 'Ahh,' he heard her say and there was light. Phyllis shone the torch around the storeroom, stacked high with boxes of Hallowe'en masks. The beam slid across to the window. *Too high and barred*. Then at the door. *Black solid oak*.

She thrust the torch on Ewan to resume her rummaging a little longer, this time fishing out a twig—

'A wand, dear,' she firmly corrected.

But it might well have been a twig for all the good it did them, sparking uselessly, first against the handcuffs, then against the lock.

'It's the iron you see, dear,' she explained. 'It's quite impossible to enchant against it.'

'A ghost can't cross it either,' added Ewan, as if further proof of the metal's strength was required.

Like Siamese twins they sat down on one of the packing cases, Phyllis preoccupied with attacking the handcuffs with a small nail file—that is until the file broke. Ewan closed his eyes. He hadn't slept for such a long while that now pure weariness overtook him. Slowly his chin dipped down upon his chest and he drifted into sleep.

Some time later, Phyllis jerked him back to his senses. 'Listen!' she hissed.

From behind the boxes came an urgent rustling sound.

'What can it be?' she asked, instinctively drawing closer to the boy.

'Mice?' he shrugged.

Phyllis gripped him in terror. 'Oh please, dear, anything but *mice*!'

The topmost boxes began to rock violently, some tumbling down.

'Not mice,' observed Ewan dryly. 'Unless they happen to be pretty big ones.'

Now, in the torch beam, something came struggling and stumbling into view. Phyllis sucked in her breath, rigid with fear, but Ewan laughed out in delight.

'Sir Edward!' he cried.

Well, he was half right.

Chapter Sixteen

Sir Edward's breastplated lower half blundered through several more stacks of boxes until, finally losing heart, it wavered and slowly sank onto the floor. As with his spirits, the starch had all gone from his elaborate ruff, making him look like a sad dejected daisy; and had he a mouth at that moment, there is little doubting his long pitiful howl of despair.

'You are acquainted with this *half* person?' asked Phyllis, astonished.

Ewan nodded. 'It's Sir Edward Upton. You kidnapped him from St Bartholomew's church, only you left his head behind.'

'I did?' muttered the vicar's wife. 'One never considers them to be detachable.'

Crouching down, Ewan gently touched the ghost's shoulder. The body stiffened, the breastplate turning left and right as if searching around, then, remembering it had no eyes to see with, the shoulders slumped down in utter misery once more.

Phyllis inspected Sir Edward closely, her glasses perched on the tip of her nose. 'Hmm, perhaps we can still do something with him,' she said. 'After all, half a ghost is better than none at all.'

'How?' asked Ewan shining the torch at her.

She shielded her face with a hand, but her lipstick had definitely curled up into a smile. 'If the key to our cell is

97

as old as the lock, it will probably be made of brass,' she said. 'And if this is so, and if the key remains in the lock on the other side of the door, your brave Sir Edward here may be able to retrieve it for us.'

Ewan was less than impressed. 'A brilliant plan,' he scoffed. 'Except aren't you overlooking one small but vital thing? How on earth can Sir Edward retrieve a key when he can't even find his way forwards to the door? He has nothing to see with—remember?'

'Perhaps,' said Phyllis, 'this is where witchcraft may finally spring to our assistance.' And with that she dramatically ripped open her handbag and took something out.

Ewan tried to see what it was, but Phyllis held it secretively to her. He sniffed, nose twitching, catching something a good deal stronger than the acrid burnt timbers around them—and overpoweringly sweet too. Instantly he recognized it as the smell of the green crystals.

'What is that stuff?' he whispered.

'Never ask a witch her age or recipes,' came the crisp reply. 'Let's just say our friends in the spiritual world find the concoction simply irresistible.'

'Like cats and catnip?' volunteered Ewan.

'A crude comparison, but yes. Like cats and catnip.'

This puzzled Ewan. 'But Sir Edward has no nose to smell with.'

'Stop being so literal and watch—'

The effect of the green crystals on Sir Edward could not be denied. His ruff visibly stiffened and his armour-plated chest seemed to swell, although Ewan realized this was impossible.

With her wand, Phyllis hastily scratched some signs in the dust.

'He's getting up!' whispered Ewan with growing excitement.

This was indeed so. Without any trace of its former clumsiness, the body of Sir Edward Upton stood up on its square-toed shoes and took its first unhesitating steps forward.

Ewan had to admit Phyllis looked remarkably impressive holding the wand in front of him, drawing him step by step closer to the door (yet careful never to touch him). On reaching the door, she simply pointed her wand and, in the best ghostly tradition, Sir Edward passed clean through: an unsettling sight to witness, equivalent to watching a swimmer who enters calm water without creating a single ripple.

'This is the more troublesome part,' confided Phyllis, kneeling down on the bare floor. With the wand she touched the bottom of the door. At the corresponding place on the opposite side they heard a gentle knock. She raised the wand a few inches higher and again, on the opposite side, a sound arose.

'Let us hope it is the good knight's hand not foot that follows,' said Phyllis, lifting the wand yet higher.

Bit by bit she lured Sir Edward up to the lock. There she did some elaborate flourishes with her wand, and they both heard Sir Edward scratching responsively on the other side.

But as the seconds crawled by, Phyllis's turns with the wand grew increasingly less elegant and more and more desperate. Ewan said that perhaps the key wasn't in the lock after all but tucked away inside Mr Hendrick's pocket. No sooner were his words spoken, however, than the clear bright sound of metal striking stone rang out. Sir Edward had done it, he had dislodged the key. Dropping to her knees again, Phyllis eagerly beckoned with her wand.

The key appeared under the door followed by several glowing fingers.

Triumphantly Phyllis snatched it up.

'Time to make good our escape,' she announced.

'Not just us,' said Ewan firmly. 'The ghosts too. We all escape together.'

The vicar's wife blinked her moist blue eyes at him. 'But they are just ghosts, dear.'

'We all escape together,' said Ewan even more firmly than before. 'Agreed?'

Phyllis hesitated longer than he thought decent, but at last agreed and Ewan told her his plan.

'Oh, how marvellously scrummy!' she cried, perking up.

She turned the key. Sir Edward was sitting on the ground outside waiting for his next set of instructions. Without stopping, Ewan seized his hand and the ghost flew up, floating behind like a balloon. They ran on, three abreast, which proved particularly awkward— especially at doors, where they were forced to manoeuvre themselves through sideways on. Luckily none of the doors was locked, and they slipped from the Hall into starlight.

'All clear,' whispered Ewan after a brief glance round.

Running low across the grass to avoid the surveillance cameras, they reached the haunted house.

'Ziggy!' called Ewan. 'Hurry—we haven't much time!'

He stepped back in alarm as a streak of silver rocketed up from beneath his feet.

'Ziggy!' he cried delightedly; then immediately grew concerned. 'Hey! Stop playing at fireworks—*he'll* see us!'

Yet Ziggy could no more keep himself still than a dog can stop a tail wagging. He flew around and around, his features blurred and lost from sight.

'Slow down,' begged Ewan. 'You're glowing too brightly.'

Ziggy flew up vertically and gently came floating back down again, until he was standing before Ewan, grinning at him, all his old confidence returned.

'I knew you'd come back for me, Ewan,' he beamed. 'I just knew that you would.'

'Not only for you,' said Ewan. 'Everyone. Listen, Ziggy, I want you to round up all the other ghosts in the park. Do you think you can have them ready to leave by the main entrance in five minutes?'

'Five?' said Ziggy scornfully. 'I can do it in three.'

'So much the better,' said Phyllis. 'And do take this headless spectre with you.'

Ziggy and Sir Edward vanished at once, and Ewan and Phyllis raced back across the grass to where Mr Hendrick's limo stood, long and dark like a hearse.

They had just reached it when Mr Hendrick rushed out from the Hall, surrounded by four or five uniformed security guards, all shining their torches at the car.

Mr Hendrick was furious. 'Mrs Flight, I warn you, go no further or I'll—'

Slipping off her red shoes, Phyllis hurled them at him, then scrambled over into the driver's seat dragging Ewan after her.

'Now go!' he cried.

Phyllis gripped the wheel purposefully, then slumped back in a crumpled heap.

'What is it?' asked Ewan.

'No key, dear, for the ignition!'

In the mirror Ewan glimpsed a soft milling ball of light rising up as high as a house, and realized that the ghosts had all assembled ready to break free. He could not let them down.

Closing his eyes he concentrated as hard as he could. *Ziggy*, he thought. *We need you to help us. Use your power—*

Ziggy's reply was instantaneous. The car spectacularly came to life with every electrical device in it working to its fullest. Windows buzzed up and down, headlights and indicators flashed, the horn blared, the windscreen washers disgorged themselves and the radio ran merrily across the dial. Ewan found himself suddenly blinking up at the roof before realizing that his seat had shot into recline, and as he lay there the car phone weightlessly floated by saying, 'The number you have dialled has not been recognized, please try again . . .'

More importantly, the engine gave a powerful roar.

Phyllis jabbed the accelerator pedal with her stockinged foot. The back of the car swayed violently and Ewan, still fumbling to rise from the vertical, was pitched across the fat upholstered seat for a second time.

'Er, you didn't happen to teach Ginnie to drive, by any chance?' he asked sarcastically.

Phyllis was silent, concentrating on her driving, steering single-handedly; her other hand still chained to Ewan's. Fortunately the car was an automatic without gears to change—and might well have lacked brakes too for all the use Phyllis made of them.

Suddenly the gates flashed into the headlights. From all sides Ewan was aware of alarm bells and shouting.

'Hold tight!' cried the vicar's wife. 'Oh, this is such marvellous fun!'

Ewan didn't understand it. The gates were there one moment—practically pressed up against his nose so to speak. The next they were smashed off their hinges and thrown forwards into the air, with barely a noise to mark their going, although a rather satisfying dent had appeared in the bonnet of the limo.

'Goodbye, Ghostlands!' he cried waving behind as they sped away.

With the ring of iron breached at last, the ghosts seized upon their chance to escape, pouring out like a glowing liquid.

Phyllis drove down the dirt track road like a woman possessed. However, no matter how fast she went, the luminous silver cloud billowing behind always managed to keep pace, lighting up the entire valley with its *ghostly* light.

Chapter Seventeen

Mrs Mulligan was closing the living room curtains against the night, when she witnessed the silver cloud rise up over the trees and descend into the garden, lighting it more intensely than daylight.

She clutched the curtains, hardly noticing the large black car that halted in the lane.

Outside, birds were singing as if for sunrise and thousands of moths and other winged insects spiralled endlessly in a light that was wonderfully soft and benign.

Finding her voice at last, Mrs Mulligan's words were little more than astonished gasps.

'Mine eyes 'ave seen the glory of the comin' of the Lord . . .'

Her lips were the only parts of her able to move.

In his study, Doctor Malthus knew nothing of this at first, looking up in bewilderment when he heard his housekeeper burst into song—

> 'What mov'd the Most High so greatly to stoop
> 'E comes from the Sky Our Souls to lift up . . .'

Dashing into the living room, the doctor peered past Mrs Mulligan's shoulder, before racing out into the garden.

The moment he stepped foot outside he began to float up, joining Phyllis and Ewan on a sparkling crest of light. For some inexplicable reason his whole body was filled with such deep happiness that he burst out laughing; and even the presence of his old enemy did not diminish the overwhelming sense of goodwill he felt.

As it was with the doctor so it was with Phyllis, and she smiled across at him. 'How glorrriously thrilling,' she purred. 'Like swimming in a pool of warm soapy water.' And she stretched herself out, giving herself over to the pure pleasure of it.

But they could not hover there all night and eventually Ewan said, 'Enough now, Ziggy. You can put us down now.'

The silver cloud started to dim; and Ewan, Phyllis, and Doctor Malthus found themselves neatly deposited on the ground.

> 'Radiance of the Light Divine
> Beam of the Eternal Beam . . .'

Mrs Mulligan sang on regardless.

'There's going to be trouble,' Ewan told the doctor. 'I doubt if Mr Hendrick will give up *that* easily.'

'Oh, he won't,' said Phyllis; and holding up her manacled hand said, 'You wouldn't have a hacksaw handy by any chance, dear?'

In the control room of Cumberforth Hall, a hunched figure sat surrounded by television monitors, each giving views of various corners of the Ghostlands complex. The TV screens were reflected in his dark glasses, but there was no expression on his face—or movement. And that stillness held something quite terrifying.

Slowly he rose, pushing back his chair. He strode across to the back of the room to a door that looked like part of the panelling. He pushed against the moulding. The door obediently opened on to a small windowless chamber. He stooped to enter. Inside, carefully pinned to the wall, were cuttings from many different newspapers. *Aeroplane crashes, motorway pile-ups, riots, famine, war* . . . He moved to the other side, to a mirrored table. Six candles were set around the mirror. He struck a match and lit them one by one with great deliberation.

The candles burned brightly. He sat before the mirror, contemplating himself through the dark glasses. Then, slowly, pulling on a finger at a time, he removed his gloves and neatly set them down. He opened a drawer and lifted out a small red casket. He opened it tenderly, as if what it contained were very precious to him. Gold glinted. Unhurriedly he selected a ring with an ugly red stone and slipped it on; then he chose another and another until rings gleamed on every finger. Slowly his jewelled hands went up to his face. He removed the dark glasses as if they were fragile and threatening to crumble; and he placed them down beside the gloves.

Again he lifted his head to view himself in the mirror. He saw his eyes burning red.

He smiled.

The security guards were struggling to lift the smashed gates when they saw the sinister figure step out on to the steps of the Hall.

'Tono! Fulmer!' They heard him roar; and above their heads stone split, shards of it dropping to the ground as if from a casting; and two fearsome creatures that might have been dogs leapt down from the gate's pillars in answer to their master's call.

As they ran they became the wind, and the wind blasted the ground, raising a scouring dust-storm that skittled litter-bins and sent papers swirling. It wrenched the trees, ripping leaves from their branches. It sent the hatless security men scrambling for cover . . .

Chapter Eighteen

Nothing whatever would persuade Mrs Mulligan to leave her place at the window, staring out across the now darkened garden in a kind of enraptured awe. Finally sheer desperation drove Doctor Malthus to pick her up bodily and, with Ewan's help, carry her up to her room.

The house was absolutely brimming with ghosts. Not that they were visible—except maybe now and again as a face in a mirror or some other polished surface. No, their presence was a sensed one. The air positively crackled; and small household objects took on lives of their own, being all too ready to rise up, or bump, or slide. But by this time nobody paid the matter great attention; for, as Phyllis herself declared, it's astonishing how quickly supernatural events can be accepted as part of the every day.

After the doctor heard a swift account of what had occurred at Ghostlands, he dashed from room to room checking all the doors and windows were locked and secured.

'Will it keep him out?' asked Ewan.

'No, but it may delay him a little.'

They then heard Phyllis urgently call out from the living room.

'I do believe he is coming!' she cried.

On reaching her side at the window, they saw the

storm's ragged edge creep steadily over the fields, visibly devouring the bright starry sky before it.

The black billowing mass moved rapidly and, as they watched, trees on the horizon, that hitherto had stood in peace, were ruthlessly blasted double, their leaves swirling away like shoals of fish.

Seconds later the poltergeist's rage struck the house like the shock waves from an exploding bomb. The initial *Boom!* hurt Ewan's ears and the walls and floors trembled; somewhere at the rear of the building glass shattered. With the wind came rain, large stinging drops, rattling like gravel against the windows. And the wind's voice quickly found its measure, becoming a terrifying unnatural howl, raising images of some great untameable beast. It so filled the ears of those inside the house, that they nearly didn't hear the urgent hammering at the front door.

'Don't answer it,' gasped Ewan fearfully. 'It can't possibly be anything good.'

The knocking persisted, refusing to be ignored.

Suddenly Phyllis's head jerked up in astonishment. 'I can hear my name,' she cried. 'I do believe . . . why, yes—it's *the girls*!'

She skidded down the well-polished hallway floor in her stockinged feet towards the front door. Ewan followed to help pull back the bolts. As soon as the last bolt was drawn, the door imploded and Bobo, Madge, and Ginnie were thrust inside, entering as a whirlwind of hair, clothes, and limbs.

After a considerable struggle, the door was eventually closed again and the storm driven back out like a frenzied animal that had tried to claw its way in. Then, turning from the door, Phyllis and Ewan were both amazed to see the chaos resulting from that single brief battle. Rugs and chairs were blown to the hallway's furthest end and all the pictures either hung crooked or lay smashed on the floor. Madge, Ginnie, and Bobo formed a heaving wet heap—Phyllis noting with satisfaction Madge trapped at the bottom.

Less a vicar's wife and more an angel of mercy, Phyllis swooped down upon her sisterhood, briskly helping them up, hugging Ginnie and Bobo in turn and then together. When she came to Madge she said stiffly, 'Your mascara's run, Madge dear.' But, overcome by magnanimity, hugged her too.

'Oh, Phyllis dear,' bawled Madge. 'Will you ever forgive me?'

Phyllis hugged her again, rubbing her back. 'Given time, Madge love. Given time.'

Bobo turned to Ewan and the doctor. 'We came as fast as we could when we heard what was happening. We thought you might be needing reinforcements.'

'Oh?' said Ewan. 'Who told you?'

By way of an answer, Bobo opened her handbag and up floated the disgruntled head of Sir Edward Upton. 'Methought you meant to keep me in confinement all eternity, madam,' he muttered ungraciously. But his mood changed almost at once when there arose a wild clattering on the stairs and his lower half came racing down to greet him. Unfortunately, in its reckless haste, it missed its footing, tripped and bumped all the way down the remaining steps to the bottom.

The head flew across and hovered fretfully over it. 'Pray, have I injured myself?' it asked with grave concern.

But the reunion soon turned into a joyful affair, the body hugging and stroking the head, and the head outrageously flattering the body—especially the turn of its legs and their ability to dance the finest galliard in three counties.

With the head once more safely tucked under his arm, Sir Edward's ghost gave the company an elegant bow. 'Thanks to you, Master Niles, I am restored whole and am wholly content for it,' he called out. 'Now, I bid thee all farewell.'

He began to fade, motioning with his hand as he did so. Sadly Ewan raised his own hand, but already Sir Edward had gone.

'Rightio, down to business,' said Madge, as practical as black lace-up shoes. 'We've brought our wands.'

'Wands?' said Doctor Malthus suspiciously. 'Why is it necessary to bring wands?'

'To lay the ghosts to rest, of course,' she replied. 'Without ghosts, that creature Hendrick will have nothing to draw his power from.'

'Splendid idea, Madge love,' agreed Phyllis.

Ewan glanced across at the doctor clenching and un-clenching his hands with uncertainty.

'We must let Ziggy go,' he said gently. 'He has to be released. It's not fair to keep him trapped here for ever.'

The doctor looked at him but did not speak.

'Come along, girls!' cried Phyllis. 'To battle!'

In the living room the witches quickly formed themselves into a circle, their wands at their feet. They joined hands and solemnly stepped one way, then stepped back again, all the time speaking the harsh ancient language of Magic.

Outside, the poltergeist knew what was happening and drove his dogs hard. Their howls grew more savage. They hurled themselves at the walls, clawed tiles off the roof, and leapt up at windows, stoving them in. Inside, candles guttered violently, a flicker away from going out.

The witches began to chant.

'In the name of the union of the four we command you to go and never return.'

The storm screamed louder, rain flooding under the doors.

Ginnie opened one eye—then both. 'It hasn't worked,' she gasped, as the air tightened about them like invisible cords.

'No,' agreed Phyllis, sliding a glance at Doctor Malthus, watching from an armchair opposite. 'Somebody is willing against us.'

Ewan ran across and shook the doctor's arm.

'Please, Doctor Malthus, you *must* let Ziggy go!'

The doctor glowered at him with such intensity of feeling that Ewan drew back.

Desperately Ewan scanned the room. 'Ziggy,' he called. 'Show us—show us that you want to be set free.'

For several seconds nothing happened, then a movement drew everyone's attention to the chimney breast. A large photograph of Ziggy had moved. It moved again; and then it unhooked itself and gently floated across to the doctor, coming to rest in his lap. Dr Malthus stared down at it and, seizing it in his arms, cradled it to him, visibly trembling.

'I can't,' he cried. 'I can't!'

Ewan touched his arm again. 'You have to.'

The doctor ran the back of his hand across his nose, then finally he nodded.

Resolutely he rose from his chair and went from the room. After a moment, they saw him pass up the hallway gripping an axe. The storm-dogs rushed in claiming the house as their own the moment he opened the front door; they went rampaging through every room, sweeping books and ornaments off shelves, slamming doors and killing candles.

At the window, Ewan and the ladies watched the doctor appear and disappear in folds of swirling grey. It was as difficult to see him as it was to comprehend his actions. But the storm needed no reason to beat him down, and he staggered, his clothes clinging to him like a drowning man. From the relative safety of the house, they saw him swing back the axe, pause, then decisively bring it down against the memorial tree; and when the first lump sprang away, the sappy flesh beneath was revealed as pale as cheese. Blow after blow followed the first, the bullying storm wilfully trying to snatch the axe from his hands or blast him off balance, but his determination proved greater than the storm's rage and the tree swayed, ready to fall.

'Oh!' gasped Bobo. 'What if it falls against the house? We shall all be crushed flat.'

'No, look!' cried Ewan, pointing upwards. 'It's Ziggy!'

They looked up to see a bright shape in the branches, seemingly caught there like thistledown.

'What on earth is it doing?' said Madge.

'He's pushing the tree away from us!' cried Ewan excitedly. 'He's pushing it away from the house!'

As he spoke they heard the ugly sound of wood

splitting and a long creak, like the creak from an unoiled door. The tree toppled with a gathering momentum, crashing diagonally across the garden.

And the moment it fell the storm abruptly died too—and in the silence came a boy's ecstatic laughter, echoing around the house, filling every room; and out across the garden where the doctor heard it, tilting back his head at the stars as the laughter went spiralling up and up, until it was no more.

Ewan rushed outside. Doctor Malthus was a grey shadow standing by a frayed tree stump. Gently the boy unpeeled his fingers and removed the axe from his grasp, placing it on the ground for safety.

In the wake of the storm's violence, the night's new-found tranquillity remained something to be marvelled at. Cautiously Phyllis poked her head out of the door before venturing further: and with her girls in tight formation at her back, she resembled a mother hen crossing the farmyard after a fox's raid. Yet there was reason for their wariness.

'Look!' shrieked Ginnie, suddenly pointing through the mish-mash of wet and broken branches. 'There he is!'

Sure enough the emaciated figure of Mr Hendrick could be observed clawing his way along the fence, his clothes swamping his dry, shrivelled body and rings dropping as golden tears from fingers that had become more like gnarled bones.

He turned on them, his eyes dull and black now, but his face screwed up with all the fury he could muster. 'I hate you as only the dead can hate the living. I hate you all! May you forever go into darkness with the terror of what may be waiting.'

He was still cursing them when his legs crumbled beneath him and he collapsed to the ground, no more than a twitching heap of rags that presently grew still.

Phyllis shuddered. 'Let that serve as a warning to us, girls,' she said. 'Now come along, we must finish this matter properly'—and with that she snapped her wand in half. Bobo and Ginnie followed her example as a matter of course. Madge lingered a moment.

'Oh, very well,' she said and broke hers too.

The pieces were scattered on the ground.

Seeing them there, the vicar's wife permitted herself a last wistful sigh.

'Oh, it'll be hard without the champagne and pearls.'

Chapter Nineteen

The morning was a time to survey damage, and repair and make good what and where they could. At first it was only the doctor and Ewan—Mrs Mulligan keeping to her room with something called *nervous exhaustion*—but before mid-morning Ginnie and Bobo arrived, bringing with them their own polishes and dusters.

A little later Phyllis and her husband pulled up in the Volvo.

'You look particularly happy today,' remarked Ewan to Reverend Flight.

He closed his eyes and smiled like a lizard in the sun. 'Why not, dear boy? Why not? It is, after all, a most beautiful morning.' Then he lowered his voice and became more confiding. 'Last night, when my dear Phyllis didn't arrive home at the vicarage and that terrible storm raged, I had an awful premonition. I feared she had been taken from me. So I prayed and prayed for her safe return; and do you know, I believe my prayers were truly heard and answered.'

'Step aside there, Rev.,' bellowed a gruff voice at that moment. 'Blocking all the pathway like a useless article.' And clumping up the lane in her wellington boots and head scarf (which made her resemble a Russian peasant) came Madge. In one hand she carried a heavy-duty mop, in the other a no-nonsense metal pail. She reminded Ewan of a knight with a lance and shield, fully armed to do battle against dirt and disorder.

On seeing what needed doing, however, Madge frowned. 'Of course,' she muttered none too discreetly, 'if we'd hung on to our wands a little longer we'd have this mess done away with in no time.'

'All with good grace, Madge dear,' trilled Phyllis, sailing by wearing a pair of pink rubber gloves.

One of the worst affected rooms was Ziggy's old bedroom above the porch. It lay squarely at the centre of the house and, as such, had suffered the full might of the storm.

The carpet squelched underfoot and a pair of rags hung limply at the shattered window. Several shelves had been brought down and toys lay strewn across the floor. Ewan held a plastic binbag while the doctor collected them up and put them inside. He smiled, handing the boy a large locomotive that had a stack which really smoked. It had been a Christmas present to Ziggy many years before.

'Of course, this room'll need completely redecorating,' said the doctor, glancing around at the damp glistening walls. 'And when it is finished, perhaps you can stay here the next time you visit me—that is, if you care to visit me again.'

Ewan nodded. 'Yes, I think I would like that,' he said.

In the garden, Ewan saw flames suddenly flare up: Phyllis was burning the poltergeist's clothes. So that she did not have to touch them with her hands she prodded them into a pile with a stick. The smoke rose thick and black.

'Good riddance to him!' called out Madge.

117

In the afternoon the glazier and builder arrived. The first was boarding up the broken windows, and the second was standing on the pathway with a stub of pencil behind his ear, sucking in his breath and saying, 'This'll cost you,' when a car urgently screeched to a halt.

To begin with, Ewan did not recognize the newcomers, until someone called out his name.

'Mum!' he cried, racing up to greet her. Mr Niles was there too, smiling awkwardly. 'Son,' he said, nodding at the boy matter-of-factly.

Prising himself free of his mother's hug, Ewan noticed his father holding a dish covered in tin foil; and he remembered the rude things he had written about Mrs Mulligan's cooking (amongst other things). He started to giggle. His parents had brought him a food parcel.

'Well, you look well enough, Ewan,' said Mrs Niles almost accusingly, after her eyes had travelled from his head to his feet and back again.

'Mum, Dad, there's been a big misunderstanding,' said Ewan. 'I didn't mean what I wrote in my letter. You shouldn't have come. Honest, I'm fine.'

Mr Niles held out the dish. 'But, Ewan, it's shepherd's pie—your favourite.'

Just then Doctor Malthus came up, and there followed the usual cordial handshakes and pleasantries, before the doctor launched into quite a convincing story about the freak storm that had caused such damage at the house. 'It's the lie of the land,' he explained. 'It occasionally throws up its own natural whirlwinds, though usually never as bad as the one we had yesterday.' And because he was a doctor, his explanation was fully accepted.

Together they strode into the house, Mrs Niles and

Ewan a few paces behind Mr Niles and the doctor who talked of old times. In the hallway Mrs Niles shivered violently.

'What is it?' asked Ewan.

'Oh, I have a thing about old houses,' she whispered. 'You know, I wouldn't be surprised if this one wasn't haunted.'

Ewan grinned broadly.

'I doubt it, Mum,' he said. 'Anyway, you shouldn't be afraid of ghosts. I'm not.'

And he looked across at a photograph of Ziggy and smiled.

Other books by Stephen Elboz

The House of Rats
ISBN 0 19 275229 4
Winner of the Smarties Young Judges Prize

The great house has become a dangerous place since the master mysteriously vanished. Wolves prowl around in the snow outside, hungry and howling, while inside the house, the horrible Aphid Dunn has taken charge. Everything seems to be falling apart.

Esther and the boys are wondering if things can get any worse, when they discover a whole new world under the house. There might still be one last chance at freedom after all . . .

Temmi and the Flying Bears
ISBN 0 19 275259 6

Temmi is furious when the Witch-Queen's soldiers come to the village to steal one of the flying bears—even more so when he discovers that they've taken Cush, the youngest cub, who is Temmi's favourite bear. Temmi is determined to rescue Cush, but instead finds himself captured and taken to the Ice Castle where he will be a prisoner, too. Escape seems impossible—unless Temmi can somehow win over the ice-hearted Queen . . .

Temmi and the Frost Dragon
ISBN 0 19 275252 9

Once again Temmi and Cush, the flying bear, are faced with terrible danger as they and their friends set out into the frozen mountains. They must reach the dragon's nest by the next full moon to complete their task, but along the way evil lurks at every turn.

But just who is it that wants their precious treasure so much that they're prepared to risk the icy anger of the frost dragon? And can Temmi and Cush ever survive this great adventure?